A CHRISTMAS NIGHTMARE . . .

"What do you want me to do?" Pam whispered, staring at the dark ground.

"I want ten thousand dollars. That's all. And I want it tomorrow night."

"But I'm trying to tell you," Pam whispered, choking out the words, "we don't have the money. . . . *Ow!*"

She screamed as both his hands dug into her waist and he pushed her into the hedge.

"Don't lie to me! I was there! I saw you!"

Books by R. L. Stine

Fear Street

THE NEW GIRL
THE SURPRISE PARTY
THE OVERNIGHT
MISSING
THE WRONG NUMBER
THE SLEEPWALKER
HAUNTED
HALLOWEEN PARTY
THE STEPSISTER
SKI WEEKEND
THE FIRE GAME
LIGHTS OUT
THE SECRET BEDROOM
THE KNIFE
PROM QUEEN
FIRST DATE
THE BEST FRIEND
THE CHEATER
SUNBURN
THE NEW BOY
THE DARE
BAD DREAMS
DOUBLE DATE
THE THRILL CLUB
ONE EVIL SUMMER
THE MIND READER

Fear Street Super Chiller

PARTY SUMMER
SILENT NIGHT
GOODNIGHT KISS
BROKEN HEARTS
SILENT NIGHT 2
THE DEAD LIFEGUARD

The Fear Street Saga

THE BETRAYAL
THE SECRET
THE BURNING

Fear Street Cheerleaders

THE FIRST EVIL
THE SECOND EVIL
THE THIRD EVIL

99 Fear Street: The House of Evil

THE FIRST HORROR
THE SECOND HORROR
THE THIRD HORROR

Other Novels

HOW I BROKE UP WITH ERNIE
PHONE CALLS
CURTAINS
BROKEN DATE

Available from ARCHWAY Paperbacks

FEAR STREET
SUPER CHILLER

R.L. STINE

Silent Night

AN ARCHWAY PAPERBACK
Published by POCKET BOOKS

New York London Toronto Sydney Tokyo Singapore

AN ARCHWAY PAPERBACK *Original*

An Archway Paperback published by
POCKET BOOKS, a division of Simon & Schuster Inc.
1230 Avenue of the Americas, New York, NY 10020

Copyright © 1991 by Parachute Press, Inc.

ISBN: 0-671-73822-4

First Archway Paperback printing November 1991

10   9

FEAR STREET is a registered trademark of Parachute Press, Inc.

AN ARCHWAY PAPERBACK and colophon are registered trademarks of Simon & Schuster Inc.

Cover art by Bill Schmidt

Printed in the U.S.A.

IL 6+

Prologue

---

*R*eva Dalby admired her reflection in the glass countertop. Only two weeks till Christmas, she thought, smoothing the eye shadow on her left eyelid with her little finger, then adjusting her wavy red hair.

Shoppers crowded the aisles of the brightly lit department store. The Christmas carols jangling out over the loudspeakers were nearly drowned out by the steady roar of voices, of shuffling feet, of ringing phones, crying babies, the whole electric buzz and whir of all large department stores at holiday time.

Reva leaned against the glass perfume counter, ignoring the blur of customers, her purple nails clicking against the glass, a nervous habit she rather enjoyed. She glanced up at the clock. Another hour until lunchtime, when she could escape from her narrow, noisy prison cell.

What am I doing here, anyway? Reva asked herself,

tapping her long nails more rapidly against the glass. Why did I ever agree to take this job?

Her cold blue eyes focused on the makeup counter across the aisle, where two salesgirls, blond model types, had scurried to wait on a dumpy woman in a stained, purple sweater-coat, carrying two brown shopping bags.

How tacky, Reva thought scornfully. That woman is beyond makeup. She should go straight to plastic surgery.

And look at the bleach job on the one over there. Or is her hair naturally green?

Reva snickered. Making fun of the customers was the only thing that got her through the day. They were all so pitiful. They just didn't have a clue.

She glanced up at the clock. It hadn't moved. I could be out enjoying my Saturday, Reva thought. She rubbed the back of her neck, then pushed her hair into place.

Why do they have to keep it two hundred degrees in here? she wondered, shaking her head. She felt as if she were suffocating. I'm going to talk to Daddy about turning down the heat, she decided.

What was that awful song on the loudspeakers? Not "The Little Drummer Boy" again! Someone should pass a law against playing that song in a public place, Reva thought, covering her ears.

She was startled by a tap on her shoulder. She spun around to see Arlene Smith, or Ms. Smith as she liked to be called, the sales manager for the perfume department and Reva's boss. She was a short, frail woman who thought she was chic and trendy because she wore men's suits.

Yuck. Those tacky shoulder pads! thought Reva. Is she going to try out for fullback for the Bears?

"Reva, do you have an earache?" Ms. Smith asked, her face wrinkled with concern.

Reva lowered her hands from her ears. "No. It's that song," she explained. "If you hear it once, it stays in your head all day and rots your brain."

"Well, I really don't think—" Ms. Smith started to scold.

But Reva interrupted her. "It's the *rum-tum-tums,*" she said. "I mean, really, how many *rum-tum-tums* can a human take in one song?"

Ms. Smith ignored the question. "Reva, I'll take the floor for a while. The Chanel reorder just came in. It's all in the back. In the cases marked Chanel. I'd like you to open them up and stock the display shelves, okay?"

"Gee, I can't," Reva said, not sounding at all apologetic. "I just did my nails this morning." She stared hard into her supervisor's eyes, as if challenging her.

"What?" Ms. Smith's small gray eyes widened with confusion. She didn't seem to believe what she had just heard.

"I don't want to wreck my nails," Reva repeated, holding up her slender hands, wiggling her fingers to exhibit the deep magenta nails. "Sorry."

Ms. Smith's expression turned quickly to anger. She sucked in her breath and drew herself up to her not-very-impressive height, glaring at Reva, obviously trying to decide how to handle this insubordination.

Gee, I hope she doesn't explode, Reva thought, forcing herself not to laugh. Her shoulder pads might fly off and hit someone.

"Reva, I'm not going to take this much longer," Ms. Smith said, her hands balled into tight fists at her sides, her voice quivering.

Just two more weeks, Reva thought. Then I'll be out of here.

She didn't say anything.

This seemed to make Ms. Smith even angrier. "I really want you to unload those cases and stock the shelves," she said, saying each word slowly and distinctly.

"Maybe later." Reva gave her a big phony smile.

"This is really the last straw!" Ms. Smith declared. She glared at Reva, then spun around on her men's wingtips and stormed down the aisle, heading toward the main-floor office.

Reva leaned against the counter and watched her until she disappeared in a crowd of customers. What's her problem, anyway? she asked herself.

My dad owns this store. He owns all of the Dalby's stores. Why should I listen to a stupid salesclerk with shoulder pads bigger than her head?

A scene across the aisle caught Reva's attention. A woman was leaning over the makeup counter while a five- or six-year-old boy tugged at her skirt. "Mom, Mom, Mom," he kept repeating, an impatient plea.

Then he tugged so hard, he tugged her skirt down to her knees. The woman calmly turned around, pulled up her skirt, and gently paddled the boy across the bottom.

Kids are a riot, Reva thought, chuckling.

"Hey, miss? Miss?" Out of the corner of her eye, Reva saw a middle-aged man in a heavy brown tweed overcoat trying to get her attention.

She carefully turned the other way, avoiding his eyes.

"Hey, miss? Miss? Please?"

Let someone else wait on him. Where was Lucy anyway? She was supposed to be back from break.

The man wandered off. Reva took out her lipstick from the drawer, pulled off the top, and twisted the tube. She turned the round countertop mirror so that she could see herself better, leaned toward it, puckered her full lips into a pout, and began spreading the magenta lipstick on them.

It took a second for the pain to register.

Then she let out a horrified shriek and dropped the lipstick.

Gasping in pain and surprise, she stared into the small mirror and saw blood pouring down her chin.

Her lips throbbed with pain.

She stood frozen in horror. So much blood! Frantically she grabbed up tissues, mopping gently at her lips.

I'm cut. I'm cut.

I can't stop the bleeding.

What has happened here?

Pressing a wad of tissues against her mouth, she saw large drips of blood on the glass countertop.

Breathing hard, she bent down and searched the floor for the lipstick tube. It had rolled under the counter. She snatched at it and brought it up to the light to examine it.

Trying to hold the tube steady in her trembling hand, Reva saw at once what had cut her.

A needle. It poked out from the center of the tube.

I've used this lipstick before, Reva thought, feeling the warm blood still running down her chin. And it was perfectly okay.

Somebody put that needle in her lipstick.

But who? Who would do such a vicious thing to her?

PART ONE

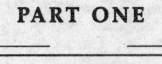

ANGRY
DAYS

Chapter 1

BROKEN UP

Two Weeks Earlier

Without warning Reva pulled the Volvo over to the curb and cut the headlights. She turned quickly toward the passenger side and watched Hank's face fill with surprise.

"Hey—" His brown eyes narrowed suspiciously. "What's the big idea?"

She studied his face as if seeing him for the first time. His hair was blond, short, and spiky. He had large, dark eyes, serious eyes. He wore a diamond stud in one ear. He had a thick football player's neck. He was big, broad-chested, with powerful arms.

Hank thinks he's tough, Reva thought.

I hope for his sake that he is.

She'd been going out with Hank Davis for more than six months, but studying him now, he seemed a stranger to her.

He's not my type at all, she thought. He's so crude, so coarse. Why did I waste so much time going out with him?

"Reva, how come you parked the car?" he asked.

I guess he was just a phase I was going through, Reva thought.

Or rather, a phase I *went* through.

She gripped the wheel with both hands and stretched. She had parked under a streetlight, the yellow light filling the windshield, making Hank's hair appear white, his skin unnaturally pale.

Beyond the streetlight she could see only bare-limbed trees, bending and shifting in a swift, wintry breeze. She must have pulled over near a small park or some woods. She wasn't sure where she was.

It didn't really matter.

"We have to talk," she said, keeping her voice low and steady, staring straight into his eyes. It sounded so cornball. This whole thing was cornball, Reva thought.

She decided to play it out for its amusement value.

"Talk? What about?" he asked, rubbing his face with his hand.

"Us," she said, making her voice dramatic, trying to sound as if she were struggling to hold back a flood of emotion.

For some reason he grinned at her. "I like that topic," he said, leaning toward her, reaching for her hand.

But she kept her hand wrapped hard around the

steering wheel. Her features tightened, and she fixed him with a cold stare. "I've decided you and I are through," she said.

Mercilessly she kept her eyes on his features. She wanted to enjoy his reaction.

A shock wave of surprise contorted his face. His eyes went wide. His mouth dropped open. "Huh?"

I guess I surprised him, Reva thought, feeling pleased. I just hope he doesn't make a big deal out of this.

Suddenly apprehensive, she felt the same sense of danger that had attracted her to Hank in the first place. He was a nice guy most of the time, she had to admit—warm, caring, kind of innocent in a way. But she liked the angry side of him too. Once, he'd punched his fist through a screen door because she refused to go to a dumb Arnold Schwarzenegger movie with him.

She had surprised herself by discovering how much she enjoyed watching him explode. Opposites attract, they say, and Hank was certainly her opposite. She was always so calm, so controlled, so thoughtful about everything she did or said.

At times she admired his spontaneity, the way he just *acted* without thinking. But more and more often lately, she found herself secretly laughing at him. He was just such a Neanderthal.

"Hey—what are you talking about?" Hank asked, rubbing the shoulder of her coat. "You mad at me or something?"

"I wish you'd stop pawing me," Reva snapped.

"No, I'm not mad at you or something. We've just had it. It's over."

He pulled his hand away and shifted his long legs uncomfortably. "What are you talking about?" She could see the anger smoldering in his dark eyes.

Maybe I should have done this in a more public place, Reva thought, glancing out at the dark trees. Not a single car had come by the whole time.

What if Hank decides to get violent?

"Let's not make a big deal out of this," she told him, rolling her eyes.

"But it *is* a big deal—to me," he insisted, a little embarrassed at having to reveal so much emotion.

Reva yawned. "It's nothing personal," she said, glancing at the clock on the dashboard: 8:06.

I've got to get this over with, she told herself. I promised Daddy I'd pick him up at the store at eight.

Daddy will be pleased that I'm breaking up with Hank, she thought. He never could understand why I went out with him in the first place.

"But *why?*" Hank was pleading. "At least tell me why."

Honey, you're too big to whine like that, Reva thought cruelly. I like you so much better when you're macho and tough.

"Hank, please—" she started, acting as if she were the injured party. "Give me a break—okay?"

"But why do you want to break up with me?" he insisted, his voice shaking as he started to lose control.

"I just decided to start the new year with someone more interesting."

What a zinger! Reva thought.

She'd been rehearsing that line all afternoon. At the last minute she had decided it was much too cruel. But—she couldn't resist.

Hank dropped back against the seat as if he'd been shot. "Whoa!" he said sadly. Then unexpectedly he lunged toward her and grabbed her shoulder angrily. "Reva, don't—"

Was he going to hurt her?

Was he going to fly out of control? Let her have it the way he gave it to the screen door?

She decided to beat him at his own game. "Let *go* of me!" she screamed at the top of her lungs.

Her outcry worked. Startled, he let go.

"You'll be sorry about this, Reva," he said, his voice trembling. He turned and stared straight ahead, unable to look at her, unwilling to let her see the emotion on his face.

Oh, brother! Reva groaned to herself. If he starts to cry, I'll puke.

"You'll be sorry," he repeated, still peering out through the dark windshield.

She popped the automatic door locks.

This wasn't as much fun as I thought it would be, Reva thought, brushing back her hair. I thought he'd at least come back at me with some arguments. I didn't think he'd sit there sniffling like a wimp and threatening me in that whiny voice.

A surprising thought crept into her mind: Maybe he really cares about me. She dismissed it quickly.

Who cares?

What do I need him for?

"Reva, you can't do this to me," Hank said, facing her finally, his features tight with anger.

"I've got to run," she said coldly. She reached across him, pulled the handle, and pushed his door open. "Take a walk, Hank."

He hesitated, staring at her with his dark eyes, angry eyes. She could see that he was thinking hard, trying to decide what to do, what to say to her.

"You'll be sorry," he said.

"Take a walk," she repeated cruelly, pressing her foot down impatiently on the gas pedal, gunning the engine.

He glared at her one last time, then slid out of the car and slammed the door behind him.

Reva switched on the headlights and shifted into Drive. She started to pull away, then stopped and slid down her window. "Oh, Hank! Hank!" she called to him.

His hands buried in the pockets of his leather bomber jacket, a grim expression on his face, he jogged slowly up to her door. "Yeah? What?"

"Happy holidays!" she said cheerfully. Then, laughing, she floored the gas pedal and roared away, leaving him standing in the street like a total fool.

A total fool!

The car hummed smoothly toward town, warm air billowing up from the heater vents. The trees gave way to brightly lit houses, many of them already decorated for Christmas.

Feeling relieved and very pleased at how it had gone, Reva relaxed, enjoying the feeling of freedom, of being by herself, of moving so smoothly, so effortlessly through the night.

I'm free, she thought. As free as the wind.

She scolded herself for having such cornball thoughts. But it was true, she realized. For the first time in six months she was free to go out with anyone. With *everyone!*

Who would she like to go out with?

She didn't have to ponder the question for long. Mitch Castelona. She'd been thinking about Mitch for quite a while.

Mitch is really cute, she thought, picturing him. His thick mop of black hair. The adorable dimples in his cheeks when he smiled. Mitch was a good tennis player. Maybe she'd invite him to the indoor tennis club she belonged to.

Yes. Mitch Castelona. A good prospect.

I'll bet I can take him away from that drippy Lissa Dewey, Reva thought with a smile.

She clicked on the radio and immediately recognized the song that came on. It was "Silent Night," a lush instrumental version. Turning onto Division Street, stores and offices rolling by on both sides, Reva began to sing along.

Such a beautiful song, she thought.

Singing loudly, she tried to block out her thoughts about Hank, but couldn't. He was having a silent night right then. He was walking all the way home in silence!

Thinking about it made her laugh again.

She was still chuckling when she reached Dalby's and pulled the silver Volvo into the executive parking lot.

The store had closed at six. Reva entered through the security guard's door. The uniformed guard was seated at a low table with his feet up, concentrating on a basketball game on the radio. He raised his eyes and, recognizing her, gave her a nod and returned to his game.

Tough security around here, Reva thought scornfully, hurrying through the narrow back corridor toward the main floor. As she stepped into the vast, empty store, dark except for a row of dim night-lights against one wall, her old fear returned.

Just chill out! she scolded herself. You're supposed to be tough.

But she couldn't control the heaviness in her stomach, the tightening of her neck muscles, the constriction of her lungs.

It wasn't fear of the dark, she knew.

And it wasn't a fear of being by herself.

It wasn't a fear that could easily be pinned down. But ever since she'd been a little girl, whenever Reva had been in the department store after closing, whenever she had walked the dark, empty aisles alone with the doors locked, the fear was there.

Cold perspiration covered her forehead.

16

Her hands felt like ice.

Her brain began to spin with crazy thoughts.

Everyone has phobias, she told herself, forcing herself to take deep breaths to slow the heavy thudding of her heart. She made her way past the perfume and cosmetics counters to the employees' elevator.

Everyone has irrational fears.

She stopped and leaned against a glass counter filled with costume jewelry. Wiping the perspiration off her forehead with the sleeve of her coat, she let her eyes wander over the store.

Nothing moved.

Silence.

Silent night, she thought.

Why am I so afraid?

She forced herself to start moving again toward the elevator against the back wall. She knew she'd be fine once she was in the offices on the sixth floor, once she was with her father.

After all, it wasn't the first time she'd met him after closing. She tried to meet him at least once a week at the store. Ever since her mother had died in a plane crash three years earlier, Reva tried to be close to her father, tried to fill just a bit of the hole that her mother's death had created in his life.

Mr. Dalby liked Reva to meet him so they could drive home together. So she forced herself to come, to walk across the vast main floor, her sneakers squeaking on the hard tile floors, her breath choking in her throat, her knees trembling so hard she could barely walk. She forced herself for his sake.

17

And because she was determined that no stupid, irrational fear would ever stand in the way of what she wanted to do.

But now the low shadows against the display cases seemed to move as she approached. Reva heard an eerie whistling sound in her ears. In the dim light everything seemed so creepy, so unreal.

What if someone has hidden in the store? Reva asked herself. It wasn't the first time the question had popped into her mind. What if a deranged person is waiting here in the dark? Or what if some disgusting homeless person is hiding here? What if some creep—

She couldn't force these silly, irrational thoughts from her mind.

And then, as she turned into the aisle that led to the elevator, a hand bumped her shoulder.

Reva gasped and spun around to face the man standing right behind her.

Chapter 2

OPPORTUNITY CALLING

"*L*eave me alone! What do you want?" Reva cried out and stumbled backward into a shelf of handbags.

The man didn't move. He just stared, wide-eyed and still.

He *couldn't* move, Reva realized. He wasn't a man. He was a mannequin.

She took a deep breath and let it out. Her throat felt dry. She was still shaking.

"Reva, you're an idiot," she said aloud, her voice sounding small in the enormous, empty store. She suddenly felt like laughing.

Of all the stupid fools. I backed into a mannequin and nearly scared myself to death!

Feeling a little better, but still scolding herself for being so weak, she stepped through the open door of the employees' elevator. The door slid closed behind her, and she pressed the button for the sixth floor.

She felt nearly normal as she stepped out onto the floor of the luxurious executive offices. The lights were all on, recessed into the dark fabric-covered walls lined with large modern paintings. Fresh flowers stood in tall vases on the plush maroon carpet. Reva passed the reception area with its leather couches and chairs and followed the hallway toward her father's office in the corner.

To her left stood a wide balcony that looked down on all five floors of the store. As she passed it, Reva peered over at the eerily silent store.

A bank of security monitors, an entire wall of TV screens, stood adjacent to Mr. Dalby's office, and to Reva's surprise, the monitors were on still, creating a low electrical hum that grew louder as she approached.

How odd, she thought. Those screens are usually turned off up here after closing.

She didn't have long to think about this. Suddenly the door to her father's office swung open, and a man in a blue uniform came bursting out, colliding with Reva.

"Oh!" she cried. She recognized the man at once. It was Mickey Wakely's dad, the store's head of security. "Mr. Wakely!"

He glared at Reva angrily, his dark eyes wild, his face and bald head bright red. "Excuse me," he said curtly and strode off without a glance back.

Still shaken, Reva saw her dad appear in the office doorway. Mr. Dalby was a trim, handsome man, dressed in an expensive tailored suit, who looked younger than his forty-five years, except for the silver that had crept along the sides of his black, closely trimmed hair.

His face usually lit up when he saw Reva. But now his expression was troubled. "Come in," he said, sighing wearily.

"Daddy, what's going on?" Reva asked, following him into the bright office. "Why did Mr. Wakely come bombing out like that?"

She sat down in a leather chair that faced her father's blond-wood desk and stared at the back of the photograph in the Plexiglas frame on the corner of the desk. She knew it by heart: it was of Reva, her little brother, Michael, and their mother on the beach in bathing suits at the Cape. The photo had been taken four years earlier, just six months before Reva's mother had been killed.

Reva always wondered why her father kept the photo there. Didn't it make him sad all day long?

"What a day," he said, leaning his forehead against the cool glass of the huge office window behind his desk. "What a day."

"So what was Mr. Wakely's problem?" Reva asked, speaking to her father's back. "He practically knocked me over."

"I just fired him," Mr. Dalby said, not turning around.

"Huh?" Her father's words took Reva by surprise. Mr. Wakely had been head of security for a long time, as long as she could remember.

She knew his son Mickey from school. He seemed

like an okay kid. He wasn't part of Reva's crowd, of course. He lived in a tiny house in the Old Village. All of Reva's friends lived near her in North Hills, the expensive section of Shadyside.

"I had to let him go," Mr. Dalby said, walking over and slumping into his leather desk chair. The chair made a soft *whoosh* as he sank into it. Mr. Dalby looked as if he had deflated too, Reva thought.

"This is just between you and me," her father said, leaning across the desk to speak confidentially to her, "but he was drinking on the job. With the holiday season coming up, I need someone who's going to give a hundred percent. I need someone I can rely on."

"He sure looked angry," Reva said, remembering Wakely's bright red face as it had loomed over hers.

"Yeah. Well . . . I was angry too," Mr. Dalby said, tapping his fingers nervously on the desktop. "I guess both of us said some things we shouldn't have. But I *had* to fire him. I really had no choice."

"You ready to go home?" Reva asked, losing interest in the subject.

"That wasn't the only thing that happened today," her father said, not hearing her question. "One of my Santa Clauses quit. Said his wife convinced him to move to a warmer climate. And I'm having all kinds of electrical problems. Christmas coming up in four weeks, and everything keeps shorting out."

"Why not use candles?" Reva suggested. "The store would look beautiful by candlelight. People would love it."

"Yeah. Till it burned down," he said sarcastically. "You've always had a *very* practical mind, Reva."

She knew he was making fun of her, but she thanked him anyway. "Only trying to get you to lighten up, Daddy." He suddenly looked a lot older to her.

"I didn't even tell you about the troubles in the Cleveland store. And the Walnut Creek store."

"I can't wait," Reva said, yawning loudly.

Mr. Dalby laughed. "Very amusing. Okay, let's go home." He started to get up, but then sank back in his chair. "Oh, wait. I almost forgot."

"Problems in the Pittsburgh store?" Reva asked.

"No. Stop being such a wiseguy."

"I can't help it," Reva cracked. "I get it from you."

He ignored her remark. "Do you have any friends who want vacation jobs?" he asked. "I already told you you can have a job this vacation. But I need four or five stock clerks. They can work weekends and part-time up till your school vacation. Then they can work full-time right up to Christmas."

"Neat!" Reva cried with real enthusiasm.

She thought immediately of Mitch Castelona. I'll call Mitch as soon as I get home, she told herself, her mind whirring excitedly. He'll be so grateful that I have a job for him, he'll drop Lissa without hesitating.

"Thanks, Daddy," she said and leaned across the desk to kiss his forehead. "That's way cool! I'll find some kids for you."

All the way home she thought about what she would say to Mitch, how she would offer him the job *and* let him know she was coming on to him.

This should be an *interesting* holiday vacation, Reva told herself. She wondered how Lissa Dewey would react when Reva stole her boyfriend from her. Just thinking about it made Reva smile all the way home.

What a hoot!

"Hi, Mitch?"

"Yeah. Hi. Who's this?"

"It's opportunity calling," Reva said, twisting the phone cord between her fingers.

"Huh? Who?" Mitch had a hoarse, croaky voice. It really didn't match his preppy good looks at all, Reva thought. It was such a comical voice, and Mitch was such a straight arrow.

"It's Reva Dalby," she said, keeping her voice low, trying to sound sultry.

"Reva? Hi. How's it going?" He sounded very surprised to hear from her. She'd never called him before.

"It's going real well," she said, rolling her eyes. She was sitting on the chair beside her bed, her feet tucked under her. "I wondered what you were doing this Christmas. Are you going away or anything?"

It took him a while to reply. He must be trying to figure out why I'm calling, Reva thought. She heard someone, a girl, ask him who was on the phone.

"No," he said finally, "I'm just hanging around, I guess."

"Well, my dad needs workers at the store. You know, Dalby's on Division Street. I told him I'd ask some people if they wanted to work. The pay is pretty good. It's part-time until vacation. Then it's full-time up to Christmas."

"Really?" he croaked.

"Think you might be interested?" Reva asked, pleased by his surprised reaction.

"Yeah. For sure!" he replied with true enthusiasm. "That's great. Yeah. Thanks, Reva. I can really use the money. You know."

"Good. I'm really glad, Mitch," Reva purred. "Maybe we can work together."

"You're going to work too?"

"Yes. I'd rather be on a beach somewhere, of course. But Daddy always has to be around for the holidays. It's his most important time of year. So I'm going to start working next Saturday morning. That's when you're supposed to start too—at eight-thirty."

"Yeah. Well, thanks, Reva," Mitch said. "This is really nice of you. I'll be there Saturday morning, eight-thirty."

She shifted the phone to her other ear, still coiling the wire between her fingers. "I'm looking forward to it, Mitch," she said sexily, hoping he'd catch her meaning. "I think we'll have some fun."

She could hear muffled whispering on the other end. Then Mitch came back on the line. "Uh—Reva?"

"Yes?"

He seemed reluctant to ask his question, but he finally got it out. "Did you say you had a lot of jobs open?"

"Well, I have a few," Reva told him.

"Do you think Lissa could work there too? She really needs the money, and she'd really like to work. You know Lissa, right?"

Sure, I know the drippy little bleached blonde with that little-girl face who everyone thinks is just so cute, thought Reva. Lissa has about as much personality as a sponge mop.

"Sure," Reva said. "I know her."

"Well, do you have a job for her too?" Mitch asked, sounding very nervous. "I mean, you can say no if you want to. But I just thought—"

No, Reva thought.

"Yes," she said. "No problem, Mitch. I'm sure Lissa can start on Saturday too."

Why not? Reva told herself, unable to suppress a cunning smile. Having Lissa right there will make it even more interesting when I take Mitch away from her.

"Hey, thanks," Mitch said happily. "Hold on a minute, Reva. Lissa is right here. I'll put her on."

What a thrill, Reva thought sarcastically.

A few seconds later Lissa's little-girl voice was in Reva's ear. "Oh, thanks, Reva. I mean, I'm so glad. Thanks."

"No problem," Reva said. "Daddy needs the help, so I thought I'd—"

"Where do we go?" Lissa interrupted excitedly. "I mean, what will we be doing? Selling or something?"

Lissa's questions gave Reva an idea, a very mean idea. She decided to play a trick on her.

26

This is inspired. *Inspired!* she thought, laughing to herself.

"Well, Lissa, wear your very best clothes Saturday morning, okay?" Reva told her, struggling to sound serious.

"My best clothes?" Lissa sounded uncertain.

"Yeah. You know. Something really sophisticated. You've got to look right. You're going to be a salesperson at one of the perfume counters. Chanel, I think."

"Really?" Lissa couldn't hide her excitement. "That's great! Thanks, Reva!"

They chatted for a few seconds more, then Reva said she had other calls to make. Lissa thanked her again, and they hung up.

Reva jumped to her feet, laughing out loud, very pleased with herself. What a hoot! she thought. I can't wait to see Lissa's face when she shows up for work in her best dress and finds out she's going to be loading shelves in the basement stockroom!

"What's so funny?" A voice startled her from her thoughts.

"Michael!" she scolded her six-year-old brother. "Don't just come barging into my room like that."

"Why not?" he asked.

She laughed. "I don't know why not!" she said. She always found it impossible to be angry at Michael. For one thing, with his curly red hair and dark blue eyes and creamy white skin, he looked just like her.

She also knew it had to be hard for someone his age to be growing up without a mother. Yvonne,

Michael's nanny, was really devoted to him and spent all her time with him, but it just wasn't the same.

He doesn't even remember Mom, she thought sadly. She watched him bouncing on her bed, using it as a trampoline. She knew she should scold him and make him go back to bed, but she didn't feel like it.

"Hey—not so high!" she cried.

"I'm flying!" he shouted happily.

Reva started to think about who else she wanted to call and offer a job. Most of the kids she hung out with were going someplace warm for the holidays.

When the phone rang, Michael let out a shriek, startling her. "Michael—that's enough," she said sharply. "Out. I have to answer the phone."

He bounced two more times, then leapt off the bed and disappeared out the door. Reva picked up the phone.

"Hi, Reva. It's Pam."

Oh, wow. It's Miss Pretty Puss, Reva thought bitterly. Miss Sweet as Apple Pie.

Pam Dalby was Reva's cousin. And even though Pam's family was poor and lived in a ramshackle old house on Fear Street, Reva, in an honest moment, would have to admit that she was jealous of her cousin.

With her straight blond hair, usually pulled back in a ponytail, and her round, friendly face, and her flashing green eyes, Pam had clean-cut, all-American good looks.

Why doesn't she wear lipstick or a little eye shadow? Reva would wonder.

Why doesn't she do something with her hair?

But secretly—and not so secretly—Reva envied her cousin, envied the way people immediately liked her, envied her ease with people and all her friends.

Of course she would never admit any of this to Pam.

And most of the time when she thought about her cousin, which was seldom, she thought of her scornfully. She was so pathetically poor, after all, and wore the same pair of jeans every time Reva saw her, and acted so . . . ordinary.

"Hi, Pam. How've you been?"

"Okay. I have a cold—but who doesn't?" Pam replied, sniffling.

I don't, Reva thought gratefully.

"How is Uncle Robert?" Pam asked.

"Daddy's fine," Reva told her. "Kind of tired. You know. It's showtime at the store."

"That's what I wanted to ask you about," Pam said. "I was wondering, Reva . . ." She hesitated. This was obviously difficult for Pam. "Uh—are there any jobs available at the store? You know. For the holidays."

No way, Reva thought, tapping her purple fingernails against the phone receiver. Who needs a poor, tacky cousin lurking about, making me feel guilty?

"Oh, I'm so sorry," Reva told Pam, making herself sound really upset. "I wish you'd called me last week, Pam. All the holiday jobs are taken."

I'm such a good liar, Reva congratulated herself. I sound so broken up, even I would believe me.

"Oh," Pam replied quietly, obviously very disappointed. "I wish I had called sooner."

29

"What a shame," Reva said, sighing sympathetically. "I really feel terrible, Pam." Then she brightened her tone. "Oh, well. Good to hear from you. We'll have to get together before Christmas. Say hi to your parents."

Reva replaced the receiver, a pleased smile on her face.

All in all, it had been quite a satisfying evening.

Pam Dalby slammed the receiver down so hard, she knocked the phone off the desk. She groaned unhappily and bent down to pick it up.

"That liar!" Pam cried out loud.

She sank down onto her bed and angrily tossed her ragged, old teddy bear against the wall. I'd love to pay Reva back someday, Pam thought bitterly.

Just once. I'd love to find a way to pay her back!

Chapter 3

A VIOLENT TEMPER

Pam picked up the phone, determined to call Reva back and tell her what she really thought of her.

What have I ever done to her? Pam wondered, sitting on the edge of the bed, staring at the phone receiver in her hand. I've always been nice to her. I've never told her how everyone at Shadyside High hates her guts.

A strong gust of wind rattled her bedroom windows. Pam felt a breeze, shivered, and reached for a tissue to wipe her runny nose.

It's no wonder I have colds all winter, she thought bitterly. This old house is so drafty.

The radiator under the windows steamed, but not much heat came up. Another strong wind gust seemed to shake the entire house.

Pam put down the receiver. What was the point of

calling Reva? Pam knew there was no way of getting through to her. She could never have an honest conversation with her cousin—Reva was too cold, too hung-up, too sarcastic to really talk to.

Reva only liked to talk about the things she owned, the fancy, exotic places she'd been scuba diving, and the boys she'd broken up with.

I can't believe two cousins can have so little in common, Pam thought. She retrieved her old teddy bear from the floor, blew a dust ball off its head, and returned it to the foot of her bed.

She still felt edgy, pent up. I'll call Foxy, she decided.

Foxy was her boyfriend and was always willing to listen to her and her troubles. It was one of his best qualities, she knew. Of course, Foxy has a lot of good qualities, she added. He's a real teddy bear too.

She started to punch in his number, then remembered that he had a social studies project to finish. Some long research paper on the Brazilian rain forest.

"Oh, well." She replaced the receiver.

I've got to get out of here, she thought.

If I have to stay home tonight listening to the wind rattle the windows and thinking about Reva and how I don't have a job and don't have a penny to spend on Christmas presents this year, I'll go bananas!

Maybe I'll borrow Dad's car and cruise around for a bit. No. That won't take my mind off anything. I'll just think in the car and end up even more angry.

She punched in a different number on the phone and reached her friend Mickey Wakely. Mickey was going to meet his good friend Clay Parker at the 7-Eleven on Mission Street. "I'll meet you there too," Pam said eagerly.

The clunky, old Pontiac Grand Prix her father had bought third-hand protested at first, but on the third try the engine did kick over. Pam let it warm up for a while, the way her father had instructed, then backed out of the gravel drive and headed down Fear Street.

It was a blustery night, clear and cold. There were a million stars overhead, and the full moon gave almost as much light as the streetlights. The wind howled like a ghost. Pam held her breath as she drove past the Fear Street cemetery, a silly superstition, she knew, but she did hold her breath every time.

As she pulled into the small parking lot in front of the 7-Eleven, Pam could see both boys through the glass storefront. Seeing them immediately made her feel better. She slammed the car door and, wrapping her wool muffler high around her neck, hurried into the store.

Mickey had a candy bar in his hand, as usual. He smiled at her in greeting, his teeth covered with chocolate. Mickey was short and very thin. He had inch-long blond hair and blue eyes and was kind of goofy looking, Pam thought, with his face full of freckles and big jug ears that stuck out a mile on either side of his head. He had a bad complexion, maybe because of all the chocolate bars he consumed, and always managed to appear awkward and uncomfortable, even when he wasn't.

Clay was also very thin, but taller and lanky. He had

brown hair that he wore slicked straight back, a mysterious scar over his right eyebrow, and steel gray eyes, restless eyes. Walking stoop-shouldered, a hard expression on his face, Clay always seemed nervous, jittery, with enough raw energy to make him ready to explode.

Pam was really fond of Mickey. They'd been friends since childhood. Until fairly recently Mickey had always been just a funny, goofy guy, always great fun to be around. In recent months, though, he'd become more quiet, even sullen. He didn't joke around as much, and he often seemed to be daydreaming, lost in thought.

Clay was Mickey's friend, so Pam tried to like him too. But there was a side of Clay that frightened her. An angry side. Clay couldn't seem to control his temper. He'd been in several fights in school and had even been suspended once for a week.

"Yo!" Clay called to her from the potato chip rack.

Mickey turned away from the candy bars. "Hey— how's it going, man?" He called everyone "man," even Pam.

"I've been better," Pam said, searching her jeans pocket for a tissue to wipe her nose. "What's happening?"

"I don't see any Zagnuts," Mickey complained, scratching his short blond hair before pawing through a shelf of chocolate bars.

"Zagnuts? Who eats Zagnuts?" Pam asked.

"They don't even make 'em anymore," Clay said, selecting a bag of barbecue-flavored potato chips.

"They don't?" Mickey looked really worried.

"Have you tried the dark-chocolate Milky Ways?" Pam asked.

"Of course," Mickey replied.

"That's his breakfast," Clay cracked.

"Hey, man, did they really stop making Zagnuts?" Mickey asked, upset.

"Why don't you write to the company and ask," Pam suggested, reading the headlines on the *Star* and the *National Enquirer*.

"Yeah," Clay said. "Write to Mr. Zagnut himself. 'Dear Mr. Zagnut, I am desperate.'"

"I don't think there *is* a Mr. Zagnut," Mickey said seriously.

Pam and Clay both laughed.

Pam glanced up to the front of the store and saw the cashier, a heavyset young guy with long, frizzy hair down to his shoulders and a thick, ragged mustache, staring at them suspiciously. "We're being watched," she told her two friends.

They both followed her glance. "Let's get out of here," Clay said, making a disgusted face.

Mickey grabbed up a few more candy bars. Clay picked up a two-liter bottle of Coke to go with the potato chips. Pam followed them to the cashier.

They dumped the items on the counter. The cashier grunted disapprovingly. "The rest of it," he said, staring hard at Clay with his little black bead eyes.

"Huh?" Clay replied.

"The rest of it," the cashier repeated mysteriously, pointing with a pudgy hand.

Clay glared back at him, his hands resting on the counter.

"What are you talking about, man?" Mickey asked.

"Empty your coat pockets, please," the cashier insisted in a low voice.

Mickey's mouth dropped open. Clay didn't move, but Pam saw that his face had turned bright red.

"They don't have anything in their pockets," Pam told the cashier.

He ignored her, his eyes leveled on Clay. "Just empty your pockets," he said wearily.

"You want to see my gloves?" Clay asked, pretending to be confused. "That's all I've got in my pockets. Just my gloves."

"Empty your pockets," the cashier repeated.

"Hey—he's some kind of miracle," Clay said loudly, turning to Mickey and pointing at the cashier.

"Huh? Miracle? What do you mean?" Mickey asked, confused.

"Well, you ever see a pig that could grow a mustache?" Clay asked. He and Mickey laughed loudly, nervously.

The cashier didn't move a muscle.

"Really. They're not stealing anything," Pam insisted shrilly. "There's nothing in their pockets."

"Ring this stuff up," Clay told the cashier, narrowing his gray eyes menacingly, leaning over the counter toward the man.

"Not till you empty your pockets," the cashier

insisted, not backing away from Clay. "Empty them now, or I call the cops. I'm not going to have you punks stealing from this store."

"Come on, man," Mickey said to Clay, his eyes suddenly wide with fear. "Let's just go." He pulled at the sleeve of Clay's cotton jacket, but Clay jerked his arm away.

"I'm not a punk," Clay told the cashier in a low, threatening voice.

"Eddie—" the cashier yelled to the back of the store. "Call the police!"

"Come *on!* Let's go!" Mickey pleaded.

"Mickey's right," Pam told Clay. "Let's just go."

"You're not going anywhere till you empty your pockets," the cashier said angrily. Then he shouted toward the back again. "Eddie—did you call?"

Clay moved so quickly that Pam let out a startled shriek.

He grabbed the cashier's shirtfront with both hands and pulled him against the cash register, hard.

"Oh!" The cashier's mouth dropped open in surprise. He raised his hands as if to protect himself.

Clay vaulted over the counter, his long legs flying, and grabbed the man again, this time by the throat.

"Clay—*no!*" Pam screamed.

Mickey took a step back, his expression frightened.

"Clay—let go of him!" Pam insisted.

But Clay didn't seem to hear her. He shoved the

cashier this time, slamming him into the cash register.

The fat cashier raised his arms in surrender, but Clay shoved him again, harder.

"Clay—*please!*" Pam begged.

Then she heard the police sirens. They seemed to be right outside the store.

Chapter 4

FASTEN YOUR
SEAT BELTS

Pam started for the door, the sirens wailing insistently. She turned to see Mickey right behind her. He was very pale, his blue eyes revealing his fear.

She saw Clay finally let go of the cashier. As the shaken man stood staring in disbelief, Clay vaulted back over the counter and ran to join her and Mickey.

A second later the three were racing across the asphalt parking lot to Pam's car. The sirens were louder now. The police had to be only a block or two away.

They piled into Pam's Pontiac, Clay taking the wheel, Pam beside him, Mickey in the back. Her hand trembling, Pam gave Clay the key. He jammed it into the ignition, turned it, and floored the gas pedal.

Nothing.

"Try it again—quick!" Pam cried.

The sirens were right behind them, on all sides of them, over them, under them. The sound seemed to be coming from inside the car!

Clay turned the ignition again, his steel gray eyes calmly staring into the rearview mirror, watching for the police black-and-whites.

The engine rumbled.

It creaked. It resisted.

Then it turned over.

Clay shifted into reverse, pulled back, shifted again, then roared toward the exit, all four tires whining in protest on the asphalt.

"The cops—they're right behind us!" Mickey shouted, his voice almost as high as the wailing siren. He was twisted around in the backseat, staring out the rear window. "I think there's only one cruiser!"

"Fasten your seat belts!" Clay cried. He tromped down hard on the gas pedal, and the big car shot forward with a jolt that sent Pam's head back against the headrest.

"Clay—stop!" she shouted. "It's my dad's car. He—"

Clay spun the wheel hard, and the car squealed, making the first sharp turn. He roared through a red light and kept going, his eyes straight ahead, not blinking, not revealing any fear, any excitement, any emotion at all.

"Wow!" Mickey exclaimed from the back. "Man, you've got this crate up to ninety-five!"

The siren was so close it seemed to be coming from the backseat. Pam closed her eyes and covered her face with both hands as Clay squealed around another corner.

"Pull over! Pull over!" came the distorted voice of an officer from the loudspeaker on the black-and-white.

"This is the police! Pull over!"

Clay laughed a high-pitched laugh. "The police?" he cried. "I thought it was Santa Claus!"

"Pull over! Pull over!"

But instead of slowing, Clay gunned the engine, pushing harder on the gas as they roared from one narrow street to another.

Pam gingerly opened her eyes and gazed at the speedometer. The needle was as high as it could go.

Clay peeled around another corner, then made a sharp right into a narrow street that a trailer truck almost totally blocked.

They're going to shoot us! Pam thought.

Just like on TV. They're going to start shooting at us!

"No!" Pam shrieked as the truck slowly pulled out from the curb in front of them.

The car was heading right for the back of it.

"Clay—*stop!*"

Instead of hitting the brakes, Clay spun the wheel. The car swerved up onto the sidewalk, missing a mailbox by less than an inch, and rolled past the truck, quickly leaving it behind, its horn honking wildly. Then Clay spun the wheel to the right, and they bumped off the sidewalk and, sailing through a red light, took the next right.

Pam struggled to catch her breath. Mickey hadn't made a sound in a long while. Clay stared straight ahead, his face still emotionless except for the beginnings of a smile frozen on his lips.

The car tore through a stop sign, then swerved past a group of teenagers crossing the street. The blocks rushed by the window in a blur of yellow light and dark shadow.

It took Pam a long while to realize that they had lost the police car.

Mickey was still silent. She turned her head to the back to see if he was okay. He was sitting stiffly against the door, staring out the window, both hands gripping the seat belt across his waist.

Clay didn't slow the car until they were a block from his house. Then, peering into the rearview mirror, he took his foot off the gas, and the speedometer needle finally began to slip back.

"Yo!" Clay screamed at the top of his lungs. "Where'd they go?"

Pam could still hear the siren ringing in her ears. She wondered if the sound would ever go away.

"Wow!" Mickey cried, finally speaking. "Wow! Wow wow wow!" He had a silly grin on his face, and his body seemed to collapse. He slumped down in his seat and let go of his grip on the seat belt.

"We lost them!" Pam cried, her heart pounding. "We really lost them!"

Clay pulled the car to the curb in front of his small redbrick house. He threw back his head and laughed with triumph, a laugh Pam had never heard before.

"Man, that was great!" Mickey declared excitedly. "Great!" He pounded Clay on the shoulder. "You did it, man. You did it!"

"When that truck pulled out, I thought we'd had it!" Pam said, squeezing Clay's arm.

"That's when we lost the police," Clay told them, his eyes glowing with excitement. "The truck cut them off—and we were *outta* there!"

All three of them laughed, a mixture of relief and victory.

"That was awesome!" Mickey declared. "Awesome!" He reached into the front seat to slap Clay a high-five. Then his expression changed. "Pam—your license plate. The police—they must have gotten the number during the chase."

"Bet they didn't," Pam replied, smiling. "The plate is off in back. It fell off last week. Dad hasn't had a chance to replace it!"

All three of them burst out laughing. They were too worked up to stay in the car. They bounded out onto the sidewalk, whooping and cheering.

"I was so scared!" Pam confessed. "I've never been that scared before!" Secretly she admitted to herself that she also found the car chase really exciting.

The wind had died down a bit, but she tightened the wool muffler around her sore throat.

Clay suddenly had a very devilish expression on his face. "Hey, guys—look what I got!" he said. He reached deep into his coat pocket and pulled out a can of jalapeño dip.

"Clay!" Pam cried, truly shocked.

Mickey gaped, swallowing hard. "You mean—"

"It was supposed to go with the chips," Clay said. He laughed and tossed the can high in the air, catching it one-handed when it came down.

"Whoa. I don't *believe* it! The 7-Eleven guy was right!" Mickey said, shaking with laughter.

"I didn't like his attitude," Clay said, grinning and twirling the stolen can in his hand.

Pam suddenly didn't feel like laughing anymore. A picture flashed into her mind of Clay grabbing the cashier by the throat and pushing him into the cash register.

Earlier, she had thought that maybe Clay was justified in losing his temper. Nobody likes to be accused of stealing.

But Clay really *had* been stealing.

Pam leaned back against the car. "You have to learn to control your temper," she told Clay softly.

He stepped toward her out of the shadows, and his face glowed under the streetlight. "Hey, I've got to have *some* fun," he said, sounding bitter.

Pam started to say something, but Mickey interrupted. "Clay is right, man. That ride we had tonight, that was the most fun I've had in years."

"But, Mickey," Pam started, "we could've been arrested. We could've been—" She didn't finish her thought.

"Big deal," Mickey said, kicking a small rock over the curb. "At least we had a little fun. You know what kind of holiday I'm going to have? My dad was just fired. Do you believe it? He worked at your uncle's

44

store for twenty-five years, and he gets fired a month before Christmas."

Pam put an arm around Mickey's shoulder and gave him an affectionate hug. "Don't mention my uncle's store to me," she said softly.

"How come?" Mickey asked.

Pam groaned. "Well, I can't even get a vacation job there."

"Huh?" Clay tossed the stolen can to Mickey, who missed. It dropped onto the street.

"You heard me," Pam said bitterly. "I said I couldn't get a job at Dalby's. My cousin said—"

"But Mitch Castelona called me just before I met Mickey," Clay told her. "Mitch said your cousin Reva was giving out jobs. Mitch got one and so did Lissa."

Pam felt her throat tighten in anger. "Reva gave them jobs?" she asked shrilly. "When?"

"Tonight," Clay told her.

Pam let out a cry of disgust. "She gave them jobs *tonight?*"

Clay nodded.

Pam furiously tossed the end of the muffler back over her shoulder. "I'm going to get Reva," she said in a low voice she didn't recognize. "I don't know what I'm going to do. But somehow, I'm really going to *get* her."

Chapter 5

REVA'S LITTLE JOKE

Reva maneuvered the silver Volvo with her left hand, leaving her right hand free to push the radio buttons. They play the *worst* music at Christmastime, she thought, stabbing quickly from station to station. If I have to hear "Grandma Got Run Over by a Reindeer" one more time, I'll scream!

It was a gray Sunday, cold and damp. The sun had come out briefly in the morning, then retreated behind a thick curtain of clouds.

Feeling tense and out of sorts, Reva had driven to her health club, intending to jog and work out for a while and then take a swim. But the pool was closed because of some sort of filter problem, and so her plans were frustrated.

Now, as she was driving past sprawling Shadyside High School, Reva wondered how she could fill up the rest of the afternoon. The tall evergreen near the main entrance to the school had been decked with twinkling Christmas lights, which were turned on even though it was the middle of the afternoon. The school was closed and dark. No sign of life.

Just six more months and I'll be out of there forever, Reva thought with a mixture of emotions, eagerness and relief, tinged with sadness. She had been accepted at Smith, her first choice, and would be heading there in the fall.

She was thinking about how senior year was turning out to be the longest year of her life when she spotted someone she knew loping along the sidewalk. Hitting the brake, she pulled over to the curb and lowered the passenger side window. "Hey—Robb!"

Robb Spring had been walking with his hands in his coat pockets, leaning into the wind, his bare head lowered. He looked up as Reva called to him and smiled when he recognized her.

"Hi!" Reva called, smiling back. She had always liked Robb. For years he'd followed her around like an adoring puppy. He was nice and funny, a lot of fun. But she'd never go out with him because he was overweight.

I just couldn't go out with such a buffalo, Reva told herself. She hadn't been very subtle about turning him down, and eventually he had given up.

She hadn't really talked with him in months. He had a girlfriend, she knew, and he was very involved with a jazz quartet he had formed. She had heard that he was a very talented pianist but had never heard him play.

"Reva, how you doin'?" He came trotting over, his breath steaming up in front of him. Robb's curly brown hair was unbrushed, as usual. His brown eyes, which always seemed to be laughing, peered into her car.

"I'm doing okay," Reva said. "How are you doing?"

He shrugged and laughed. "Okay, I guess. Just running some errands for my mom."

"You're such a good boy, Robb," she teased.

"I can be bad too," he replied suggestively, leaning into the car with his head lowered.

They chatted for a while, catching up. Then, as they talked, Reva had an inspiration.

Robb would make a great store Santa, she thought. Daddy said one of his Santas quit and he needs a replacement. Well, Robb would be perfect. He's so jolly. He has just the right personality for it. And he's so roly-poly, he wouldn't even need any padding!

"Hey, Robb, do you need a job this Christmas?" she asked, pleased as she thought about how happy her dad would be with her.

"Yeah. I guess," Robb said. "I planned to pick up some money shoveling driveways for people. But it's been a little slow . . . since it hasn't snowed. I offered to shovel anyway. You know, for half price. But no takers." He grinned at her, his round face pink from the cold.

"No. I'm serious," Reva said. "My dad said I could hire some people to work at the store. You know. Dalby's."

"Really?" His expression turned serious. "Well,

48

that would be excellent, Reva. You know, things have been tough at my house. We could really use the money."

"Well, great," Reva said. "You can start Saturday."

"For real?" he asked.

"Yeah, for real," she told him, wondering why he never brushed his hair. She suddenly had another idea. Why not play a little joke on Robb too? He had a good sense of humor. He'd appreciate it. Eventually —maybe.

"Listen, I have a special job in mind for you," she said, picturing him in a Santa Claus suit.

"Huh? What kind of job?"

"It's a—uh—public relations job," she said.

He looked doubtful. "Public relations? I don't know anything about public relations."

"Don't worry," she assured him, "you'll be great at it. Really." She couldn't wait to see him sitting on Santa's enormous throne with a sticky-fingered kid sitting on his lap, pulling at his white beard.

His dark eyes were lit up with excitement. "Thanks, Reva," he said. "This is really nice of you."

"See you at the store. About eight-thirty," she said. As he thanked her again, she pushed the button to roll up the window and headed down the street.

What a hoot, she thought.

She couldn't wait till Saturday morning. Robb would show up in a suit and tie, no doubt, ready to begin his important public relations job—only to be handed a bright red Santa costume, complete with beard, wig, and stupid pointy hat. And Lissa would be standing there in her glitziest dress and be sent to the stockroom to unload boxes and stock shelves.

They'll be mortified, Reva thought, grinning from ear to ear. Mortified!

Congratulating herself on her cleverness, she pulled into her driveway, heading along the row of tall hedges to the four-car garage in back.

That night, Reva's father went out, leaving her to baby-sit for Michael. She played an endless hour of Chutes & Ladders with him, then settled him down with a cartoon tape on the VCR so she could have some time to herself.

She didn't get him to bed until nearly ten, more than an hour past his normal weekend bedtime. He seemed nervous and clingy and kept making up excuses not to go to bed.

The poor guy is lonely, Reva thought. But what am I supposed to do about it? An entire hour of Chutes & Ladders is cruel and unusual punishment!

Finally Michael agreed to be tucked in only on the promise that Reva would wake him when their father got home so that he could say good night to him. Reva promised, with her fingers crossed, turned out the light on his dresser, leaving only the night-light on, and crept downstairs.

He's sweet, but he's a pest, she decided. I can think of better things to do at night than this.

She suddenly thought of Mitch Castelona and wondered what he was doing right then.

Out somewhere with Lissa, no doubt.

Well, enjoy it while you can, Lissa, Reva thought. In a few weeks *you'll* be the one sitting home—while I'm out having fun with your precious Mitch.

She picked the new issue of *Vogue* up off the coffee table and sat down in a big, overstuffed armchair by the fireplace to thumb through it. She was nearly done, having stopped to read only photo captions, when she heard a loud knock on the door.

"Oh!" The sudden barrage of sound startled her.

She turned toward the front hall. Who could it be this late?

She hurried to the front hall and put her face close to the door. "Who is it?" she called.

No reply.

"Who is it?" Reva repeated, listening hard to the silence, suddenly filled with dread.

Chapter 6

SURPRISE ATTACK

"**W**ho's there?" Reva repeated sharply.

"It's me," a voice said finally. A boy's voice. Hank's voice.

She made a disgusted face and reluctantly pulled open the door. A cold rush of air blew into the room as Hank, smiling, walked past her into the entryway.

"Hank, what do you want?" Reva asked coldly.

He wore a bulky, fifties-style overcoat, unbuttoned, revealing a gray sweatshirt underneath. His spiky, blond hair caught the light from above.

He continued to smile warmly at her, as if nothing had happened between them, as if she hadn't broken up with him so cruelly. "Can we talk for a few minutes?" he asked almost shyly.

"What for?" Reva asked, blocking his way into the living room.

"I-I've been trying to call you," he said, his expression serious. "I left messages on your machine. You didn't call me back."

"I know," Reva said, rolling her eyes. "Maybe you should've taken the hint."

She walked past him to the front door, pushed open the storm door, and held it for him. "Good night, Hank."

He brushed past her and went out onto the front porch. "I just want to ask you something," he said quietly, avoiding her eyes. "A favor. Not about us. Okay?"

Warily she followed him out onto the porch but didn't say anything. Another blast of cold air made his heavy overcoat flap noisily. He pulled it tighter.

"What's the favor? Hurry up. It's freezing," Reva said impatiently.

"I'm sorry, Reva. This isn't easy for me."

"What do you want?" Reva asked, unwilling to soften her tone. What was he doing here anyway? She was finished with him. Finished.

"I—uh—heard you were giving out jobs. I—uh—wondered if there are any left," Hank said, blushing. "You know. At your father's store."

Reva laughed cruelly. "For *you*?"

"I could really use a job, Reva. This was hard for me—to come here tonight. You know? Okay, so you don't want to go out with me anymore. All right. But if there are jobs available, I thought . . ." His voice trailed off. Reva's cold glare wasn't making it any easier for him.

"I don't think so, Hank," she said quietly.

"Huh?" He stared at her, not believing her casual cruelty.

"I don't think so," she repeated, not bothering to hide her amusement.

With an angry cry he grabbed her arm. "What is your *problem?*" he screamed.

"Let go of me," Reva ordered.

But he gripped her arm even tighter. Seething with anger, he glared at her. "Why are you doing this to me?"

"Let go!" she cried, more angry than frightened. And then suddenly she put her teeth together and whistled, a piercing, high-pitched, steady tone.

Hank's eyes opened wide in surprise, in confusion, and he dropped her arm.

A second later the shrubs beside the house began to rustle.

Then they both heard a low growl, a frightening sound that rapidly became louder, closer.

And roaring out of the darkness came King, the Dalby's guard dog, their well-trained Doberman, obeying his attack signal, Reva's whistle.

The dog had ignored Hank earlier because Hank was a familiar guest at the Dalby house. But now this was the signal. Time to attack.

The dog's eyes flared red. Then, snarling with automatic rage, the enormous Doberman raised its powerful front paws and leapt against Hank's chest.

Hank cried out, stumbling two steps backward. "Reva—stop him!"

Ignoring Hank's cries, Reva moved away, her eyes wide with excitement.

The snarling dog snapped its jaws against the sleeve of Hank's overcoat.

Hank jerked his arm away, gained his balance, and took off across the lawn. The dog followed, furiously leaping at Hank's back, biting at Hank's legs.

Reva watched from the porch, waiting until Hank was all the way to the street before she gave a second whistle, signaling the dog to cease its attack.

Hearing the whistle, the Doberman stopped in its tracks as if its Power switch had been turned off. Panting loudly, it turned and stared expectantly up the lawn at Reva.

Hank pulled open his car door and started to climb inside. But realizing his attacker had been called off, he stopped and, holding on to the car door, stared back at Reva.

She could see the anger on his face illuminated by the light from inside the car.

"I'll pay you back!" he yelled. "Reva—do you hear me?"

Reva laughed scornfully. "Don't you like to play with King?" she called. She tilted her head back and whistled loudly again.

Instantly the Doberman sprang to life, deep growls signaling its violent intent.

Reva watched as Hank dove behind the wheel and slammed the car door. A few seconds later he peeled away, leaving the howling, disappointed attack dog at the curb.

Reva hurried back into the house, closed and locked the door behind her. She shivered.

Hank was so ridiculous, she thought. The *look* on his face when he realized the dog was after him!

What a laugh! Reva thought. What a laugh!

Chapter 7

REVA GOES TO WORK

Reva tried to suppress it, but she couldn't help herself. She tossed back her head and let the laughter escape.

The other stock clerks in the employees' lounge turned to see what the commotion was. Lissa glared at Reva, then at Mitch. Then her face turned crimson, and she held her hands up to her face and gasped.

It was eight-thirty Saturday morning, and Lissa had just arrived for work wearing a gray wool skirt, silk blouse and blazer, and high heels. Before even saying good morning she noticed that the other workers were in jeans and sweatshirts and sneakers.

"Reva, what's going on?" Lissa asked, her eyes surveying the others, who were now all staring back at her.

Reva, trying to keep a straight face, started to answer, but before she could say a word, Donald

Rawson, the head of the stockrooms, walked over to Lissa and scowled at her.

That was when Reva lost it. She started to laugh.

Lissa, blushing hard, turned to Mitch for support. Reva could tell by the expression on Mitch's face that he felt really bad for Lissa, but he avoided Lissa's glance and didn't say a word.

"We generally tend to dress down a bit in the stockrooms," Donald Rawson told Lissa, rubbing the top of his bald head.

"I—I thought I was going to be at a perfume counter," Lissa stammered. "I mean, Reva told me to dress glitzy, and—" She glared at Reva.

"I'm so sorry, Lissa," Reva gushed. "I guess I got the information wrong. Can you *ever* forgive me?" Reva was dressed conservatively in a straight skirt, navy blue sweater, and pearls.

Some of the other stock clerks giggled loudly across the room.

Rawson flashed them a warning frown. "Miss Dewey, perhaps you'd better go home and change," he suggested to Lissa. "But hurry back. Several trucks came in this morning. We have a lot to uncrate today."

Lissa gave Reva one last angry glance, then bolted from the room, her high heels clicking across the concrete floor.

Almost as soon as she disappeared out the door. Robb entered, peering around the small room uncertainly. He was dressed in a brown wool sports jacket dark brown slacks, a white shirt, with a green- and brown-striped tie.

He had a bright red Santa costume draped over his arm. He searched the room, spotted Reva, and angrily marched up to her.

"Reva—if this is your idea of a joke, it isn't very funny," he said, gesturing with the costume.

The hairy white beard fell to the floor, and when he bent down to pick it up, the Santa hat fell. Everyone was laughing.

"I don't believe you. I really don't," Robb said to Reva, ignoring them.

"Robb, lighten up," Reva said, enjoying his distress immensely. "You're perfect for Santa. You won't even need any padding!"

More laughter. Robb's mouth dropped open, but no sound came out.

"Reva, I see you're up to your old tricks," Donald Rawson said, shaking his head with disapproval.

"Who? Me?" Reva asked with exaggerated innocence.

"We've got to get to work," Rawson said sternly, glancing up at the large wall clock above his head. "The store is opening at nine-thirty." He turned to Robb, who was standing still and breathing heavily, obviously very upset. "Are you going to put on the costume?"

"I guess so," Robb said grudgingly. "I'd like to forget the whole thing, but I really need the money." He sighed. "Maybe it'll be fun."

"You were born to play this part," Reva said enthusiastically.

"That's enough, Reva," Rawson said sharply. "Isn't it time for you to get to the cosmetics counter?"

"You're a salesperson?" Mitch asked, surprised, the first words he had said all morning.

Reva nodded with a smile. "Daddy wanted me to start at the bottom. But I refused."

"Reva, *please*—" Rawson snapped. "I have to give the new workers their assignments." He raised the clipboard he'd been holding at his side.

"Before I go upstairs, I just wanted to speak to you for a moment," Reva said, grabbing Rawson's arm and pulling him aside. She held on to the clipboard and studied it for a moment. Then she leaned forward and whispered confidentially to Rawson, just loud enough for Mitch to overhear. "I want to make sure that you put Mitch and Lissa in different departments."

She watched Mitch's eyes light up, then turned back to Rawson. "I see you've already done that. Thanks." She let go of the clipboard and started toward the door. "See you later, Mitch," she called softly, giving him her sexiest smile.

Reva headed along the narrow corridor toward the escalator that would take her to the main floor. What a morning! she thought, very pleased with herself.

Her little jokes had gone off even better than she could have hoped. Lissa's face turned red as a tomato,

Reva thought, chuckling. Maybe it'll never go back to its natural pasty color!

What a drip.

Mitch will be much better off without her. She's such a waste of time.

The little surprise she had cooked up for Robb had gone really well too. She had to laugh. There he was, ready to begin a management career, but the only thing he was going to manage was a line of drooling kids from a chair in Santa Land.

She probably shouldn't have played those jokes, Reva thought. But why not? Why not get a few laughs?

Besides, Mitch, Robb, and Lissa were all lucky to have jobs.

Despite her jokes, Reva was certain they were grateful to her.

Of *course* they were grateful. They had to be.

Everything was going so well. Reva had seen on Rawson's clipboard that Mitch was assigned to electronics, Lissa to the book department.

Hope she doesn't get too many paper cuts opening the book cartons, Reva thought nastily.

She knew that Mitch had overheard her request to Rawson, so he had to know that Reva was interested in him. She hadn't been very subtle about it. But subtle wasn't Reva's style.

Later, she decided, she'd pay a visit to Mitch and be even *less* subtle.

Yes, this was definitely starting out to be fun.

Walking jauntily, Reva was just a few yards from

the escalator when a hand grabbed her from behind and pulled her roughly around the waist.

"Hey!" she cried, trying to pull free. "Let go—"

Another hand clamped hard over her mouth.

Despite her struggles, she found herself being dragged into a darkened supply room.

Chapter 8

A LITTLE SCARE

Reva's heart thudded in her chest. Her eyes struggled to adjust to the sudden darkness. She couldn't break away. She couldn't scream.

Then, to her surprise, the hands that had pulled her into the empty room loosened and let her go.

Reva spun around, anger overcoming her fear.

"Hank!" she cried. "What are *you* doing here?"

He laughed that familiar, high-pitched laugh. His dark eyes glowed in the dim light of the supply room, his expression mirthful, amused.

"Did I give you a little scare?"

She stared back at him, unwilling to let him know just how much he had terrified her.

"Just paying you back for Sunday night," he said, still grinning, his face close to hers.

"What do you want?" she snapped, edging back toward the open door. "Did you come here just to pull that dumb joke?"

His smile broadened. "I work here," he said.

Reva's mouth dropped open in surprise. "Huh?"

"You heard me. I work here. Starting this morning."

She took another step toward the door. "You got a job here? Someone hired *you?*"

His smile faded. His eyes burned into hers. "I didn't need you to get a job. I did it on my own."

She uttered a scornful laugh, twisting her face into a sneer. "So where's your broom? Or did they only issue you a dustpan?"

He didn't react to her sarcasm. "I'm working in the security department," he said quietly. "An assistant. I watch the security monitors."

Reva shook her head scornfully. "Perfect job for you, Hank. Watching twelve boob tubes all day long and getting paid for it."

He jammed his large hands into his jeans pockets. Her remark had gotten to him. "Hey, you know I'm into electronics," he said, sounding defensive. "Who fixed your VCR last week?"

"Who fixed your *brain?*" Reva cracked. "You're just following me around, Hank. That's the only reason you got a job here. You can't believe that I broke up with you. But I did." Her voice hardened, her eyes grew cold. "It won't do you any good. We're through, Hank. So leave me alone."

As much as he tried to conceal it, Hank's face revealed that her words had stung him. "I needed a job. That's all," he said but without conviction.

Then he grabbed her arm. "Listen, Reva—"

"Let go!"

"I didn't do anything to you," he said heatedly. "You have no reason to give me a hard time."

"Let go. You're *hurting* me!" she cried.

He let go of her arm but didn't back away.

He's so big, Reva thought, so powerful, so strong. If he really wanted to hurt me, he could do it easily.

"I'll be watching you, Reva," he said with sudden menace.

"What?"

"I'll have twelve monitors. I'll be watching every move you make."

Even in the darkness of the empty supply room, Reva could see his anger. As she backed away from Hank into the corridor, his words echoed in her mind and she felt a chill, a cold tingling down her spine— the chill of real fear.

"Clay, what's with the knife?" Pam asked.

He shrugged. "Just playing." He continued opening and closing the blade.

He always has to be fiddling with something, Pam thought, watching his hands. He can never just sit still.

"Hey, man, that's not a Boy Scout knife," Mickey said, scratching his head. "Where'd you get it?"

"Found it," Clay said, an odd smile forming on his lips.

They were sitting in Mickey's small, boxlike living room. Pam slouched low in the worn cushions of the threadbare couch, Clay in the wooden chair across from her, Mickey on the floor, his back against the couch, his legs stretched out straight in front of him, two unwrapped candy bars in his lap.

Across the room the TV was on, a rerun of some police show. No one paid any attention to it. The wind howled outside the narrow living-room window, rattling the glass.

The sound of a pop-top being pulled could be heard from the kitchen just behind the living room. They could hear Mr. Wakely shift in his chair at the kitchen table. He'd been sitting there since Pam had arrived, finishing off two six-packs of beer. She'd heard him get up once to go to the refrigerator and pull out another six-pack.

"He's been drinking nonstop ever since he lost his job," Mickey confided, lowering his voice to a whisper. "He's heartbroken. I can't even talk to him about it."

"Has he tried to find another job?" Pam whispered.

Mickey shook his head. "He hasn't left the house. Except to buy beer."

"Some Christmas this is going to be," Clay said glumly, slapping his palm with the side of the knife blade.

"Where's Foxy?" Mickey asked, tearing open one of the chocolate bars and taking a big bite.

"He had to work late tonight and then go someplace with his parents," she replied, her fingers playing with a ripped bit of fabric in the arm of the couch. "You know he got a job."

"Huh? Where?" Mickey asked, chewing.

Pam rolled her eyes. "At Dalby's. Do you believe it?"

Clay snickered bitterly. "Foxy got a job at your uncle's store and you couldn't?"

Pam's expression darkened. She could feel the anger building inside of her, like a volcano ready to explode. "I have my cousin Reva to thank," she said through gritted teeth.

"She's a cold wind," Clay said, twirling the knife in his hand. He smiled, pleased at his poetic description.

"She's a liar. That's what she is," Pam said heatedly, surprised at the force of her own emotion. "Someday I'm going to tell her what I think of her."

"Why not do it right now?" Mickey suggested, gesturing toward the phone on the low table beside the couch.

Pam considered it briefly, then shook her head. "It's not worth it. First thing you know, Uncle Robert would be calling my dad, and it would start a big family fight."

"So?" Clay asked, staring at her with his hard, steel gray eyes.

"So I don't want to wreck my parents' Christmas too," Pam told him, still playing with the frayed couch fabric. "I don't want to start a world war. I'd just like to get back at Reva somehow."

From the kitchen they could hear the top being popped off yet another beer can. "I hate your uncle too," Mickey said angrily. "Look at what he did to my dad. A month before Christmas."

Clay burst out humming a loud, off-key version of "Deck the Halls," twirling the knife as he sang. He stopped abruptly and jumped to his feet, the diamondlike stud in his ear catching the light from the floor lamp. "Can you guys keep a secret?"

Pam gazed up at him. She'd only seen that gleeful expression on his face once before, when he'd ditched the police cruiser.

"Yeah, sure," Mickey said, pulling himself up straight.

"No. I mean it. Really," Clay said, starting to pace quickly back and forth across the small room.

Mickey pulled himself up beside Pam on the couch. They both followed Clay with their eyes, wondering what had gotten him so worked up. "What's your secret?" Pam asked.

"Come on, man. You know you can trust us," Mickey added.

Clay stopped pacing and leaned against the windowsill, staring out into the darkness. "I've been working on a little plan," he said quietly, so quietly they had to struggle to hear him.

They waited for Clay to continue. But instead, he walked over to the TV and turned up the sound. Then, glancing toward the kitchen, he pulled the wooden chair over to the couch and straddled it right in front of Pam and Mickey.

Hugging the chair back, he began to speak in a low, excited voice, glancing toward the kitchen every few seconds, obviously determined that Mr. Wakely wouldn't hear what he was saying.

"I have this plan," he repeated. "I know it'll work. It's a way we can have a good Christmas. I mean, get presents and stuff." He glanced nervously toward the kitchen, then turned his eyes on Pam. "And it's a way you can get back at your cousin."

"Huh?" Pam stared at him, confused. "Clay, what are you talking about?"

"I've already worked it out with the night security guard at Dalby's," Clay whispered excitedly, leaning close to Pam and Mickey. "I'm going to rob the store."

Chapter 9

THE PERFECT CRIME

"Maybe you two would like to come along?" Clay asked.

Mickey laughed and playfully slapped Clay's shoulder. "You're kidding, right?"

But Pam knew immediately that Clay was serious. Clay, she knew, didn't really have a sense of humor. He didn't kid around or say things to get a reaction from people.

Clay meant what he was saying.

The intensity on Clay's face quickly convinced Mickey that Clay really was planning to rob Dalby's. And now Clay continued to stare expectantly at both of them, as if awaiting an answer.

"Hey, Clay, come on!" Pam exclaimed. "I can't rob my own uncle's store!"

Clay's eyes filled with alarm, and he stood up to

clamp a hand over Pam's mouth. He peered toward the kitchen, listening for any sign that would indicate Mr. Wakely had heard. Then, slowly, he pulled his hand away from Pam's face.

"Sorry," she whispered. "I forgot."

"Don't sweat my dad, man," Mickey assured Clay. "He's so out of it, he doesn't know what's going on."

"Let's just keep it down anyway," Clay said sharply. He sat back on the chair, his long arms dangling over the chairback, his legs straddling the seat. "Listen, Pam, it won't be like an actual robbery," he explained. He opened his knife and began tapping the blade against his open palm again. "It'll be sort of like Robin Hood. Know what I mean? We'll take some stuff from the rich and give it to the poor for Christmas—namely us."

Mickey giggled again, nervous laughter. "I don't believe you, man."

"Well, believe it," Clay said seriously, tapping the knife blade harder against his hand.

"I can think of easier ways to get back at Reva," Pam said, this time remembering to whisper.

"Yeah," Mickey said, scratching his jaw nervously. "Robbing a big department store could be dangerous, you know?"

The wind picked up, rattling the window hard. Clay whipped his head around, as if expecting to see someone standing behind him. Seeing no one, he turned back to his friends, his expression still hard and serious.

"It's not going to be dangerous at all," Clay said in a flat, expressionless tone. "It's not even going to be a real robbery."

"What are you talking about?" Pam asked.

A chair scraped across the floor in the kitchen. Mr. Wakely let out a groan. Clay raised his hand, signaling the others to be quiet. A few seconds later they heard quiet snores from the other room. Mickey's dad had fallen asleep.

"I know John Maywood," Clay said, relaxing a little as the rhythmic sound of the snoring continued to float into the room. "He's the night security guard. He's an old friend of my dad's. Your dad must know him too, Mickey."

"Yeah. Sure. I know who John Maywood is," Mickey said, shifting uncomfortably on the couch.

"Well, Maywood is real sore that your dad got fired," Clay told Mickey. "When I told him I had this idea about robbing the store, Maywood just laughed. He thought it was an excellent idea. He hates the Dalbys. He said right away that he'd help me."

"Help you? How?" Mickey asked.

Pam sat staring at Clay in silence, wondering how far Clay really would go with this, wondering how far he'd *already* gone.

"Maywood said he'd open a back door and let me in. Then he said he'd let me take whatever I wanted. No problem. He'll even stand guard for me."

"Wow!" Mickey exclaimed, twisting the candy-bar wrapper in his hand. His expression became thoughtful as he considered everything Clay had said.

"Won't Maywood lose his job?" Pam asked. "Won't the police know right away that he let you in?"

"Not if I make it look like a real robbery," Clay replied excitedly.

"You mean—"

"I mean, I have to make it look like I knocked him out or something. Maybe tie him up. Hit him over the head. You know. Just hard enough to make it seem real. Maywood said he could handle it from there."

"But what does he want in return?" Pam asked suspiciously. "He's not going to go through all this to help you rob the store just because he hates my uncle so much."

"No. You're right," Clay said quickly. "He has a list. You know, some things he wants me to steal for him. Not a whole lot. Just some stereos and a fur coat. Toys for his kids."

"This is crazy, Clay," Pam said. "It's just crazy."

"What about the alarm?" Mickey asked. "Is Maywood going to help with that too?"

Clay nodded.

Pam could see that Mickey had already cast aside any doubts and was ready to join Clay in this plan.

In a way she couldn't blame Mickey. She knew how upset he was seeing his dad fired like that and then watching his dad fall apart the way he had.

She could understand Mickey's desire to carry out a plan that would avenge his father.

Pam had a lot of the same feelings.

Not just because Reva had lied to her once and said there were no vacation jobs at the store. It wasn't the first time Reva had lied to her, had kept her down, had made sure that Pam knew her place. Their entire lives, Reva had treated Pam as an inferior, as a poor relation, as a nuisance to be snubbed, to be looked down upon, to be taken advantage of.

Well, thought Pam, maybe Reva hadn't been like that for their *entire* lives. There *had* been a time when they were friendly, when they confided in each other, when they did things together.

All that had changed when Aunt Julia, Reva's mother, had died.

Everything changed. Especially Reva.

She had cut off any close ties they had had. Overnight she had turned cold to Pam, had become cruel and superior.

Is she angry, Pam wondered, because my mother is still alive and hers isn't?

No. That was too crazy. The idea that Reva, who had everything, could be jealous of Pam was just too absurd. Pam refused to believe it.

But then why was Reva always so horrible to her?

Pam realized that in the past three years she had grown to hate her cousin. Reva's refusal to let Pam have a job was the final straw.

The final straw. . . .

To Pam's astonishment, she found herself seriously considering Clay's plan.

"But how do we get into the safe?" Mickey asked. "Maywood can't get us into the safe, can he?"

"No. No safe," Clay told him flatly. "We're not going to steal money. I promised Maywood that. We'll just take clothes, and radios, and CDs, and stuff. Anything we want for Christmas."

That bit of information made Pam feel a little easier. Robbing a safe seemed much more serious than grabbing some jeans and CDs.

"And there's no way the police will know we've been there?" Mickey asked.

A loud snort from the kitchen made all three of them jump. They froze, listening hard until the regular and gentle snoring resumed.

"There's no way the police will know," Clay assured Mickey. "If the alarm doesn't go off, the police don't come. And Maywood told me he won't trip the alarm till we're gone."

"And then," asked Mickey, thinking hard, "when the cops finally do show, Maywood tells them he didn't see anything? He can't identify us?"

"That's right," Clay replied, a grin slowly forming on his narrow face.

Pam saw that Mickey was grinning too. "Neat!" he exclaimed. He turned to Pam. "It's an excellent plan, isn't it?"

Pam shook her head. "I don't know," she said softly.

"Come on, Pam—" Mickey urged.

"There's no danger. Really," Clay told her.

"And think of how much you hate your cousin. Think of all the presents you can't buy because she wouldn't give you a job. Think of how rich she is and how poor you are."

"No!" Pam cried suddenly and jumped to her feet.

Both boys were startled and jumped.

"No," Pam repeated. "I couldn't do it. I just couldn't rob my own uncle's store." She walked over to the window and peered out past her own reflection in the dark glass. A storm of wet sleet had started. "I'd be too afraid anyway," she added.

"Okay, okay. That's cool," Clay said, raising both hands in a gesture of calm. "You don't have to be part of the robbery."

"Good. Because I won't be," Pam said emphatically.

"But maybe you could just drive Mickey and me there," Clay suggested.

Pam realized he had this all worked out. He probably figured Pam would refuse to help, but Pam was the only one who had a car. He needed her.

Pam, suddenly chilled, moved away from the window. "What are you asking me to do, Clay?"

"Just drive the car." He raked a hand through his brown, slicked-back hair. "Just drive us there. And wait for us. The trunk on that old Pontiac of yours is big enough to hold an elephant. We'll stash the stuff in there, then bring it to my house."

"You want me to drive the getaway car?" Pam cried dramatically.

"There won't be anything to get away from," Clay reminded her patiently. "No one will be chasing us, remember?"

Pam swallowed hard. "Okay. I'll do it," she said. And then she thought—did I really say that?

Did I really just agree to drive the car for a robbery?

It isn't really a robbery, she told herself. Besides, if anything goes wrong, Uncle Robert won't press charges against me.

At least, I don't *think* he will.

A knock on the front door startled them all. Pam cried out. Clay nearly toppled off the wooden chair.

"Oh. That's Foxy," Pam said, her heart still pounding. "I forgot. I asked him to pick me up here."

She started for the door, then stopped and turned back to the two boys. "Be quiet about this. I don't want Foxy to know."

They both nodded in agreement.

Foxy was a nice guy, and a bit of a straight arrow. He definitely wouldn't approve of Clay's plan. Especially since he had just started working at Dalby's too.

Pam pulled open the door, and Foxy hurried in out of the sleet and raging wind. "What a storm!" he cried, shaking the water off like a dog after a bath.

"Hi, Foxy." Smiling, Pam led him into the small living room.

"Hey, man—how's it going?" Clay asked.

Foxy, his dark hair drenched and matted against his head, shrugged his broad shoulders. "You know."

"How was work?" Pam asked, searching the closet for her winter coat. "Did you see Reva?"

Foxy groaned. "Yeah, I saw her. Let's talk about something pleasant instead."

As Foxy took a seat by the window, Pam found her mind wandering back to the robbery plan.

It's nothing to worry about, she thought.

It's going to be so easy.

Clay has it all planned so perfectly, what could go wrong?

Chapter 10

KISS, KISS

"You're so lucky, Pam," Reva said, wedging the phone receiver between her chin and her shoulder so she could let her newly polished nails dry.

"Huh?" Pam reacted on the other end of the line.

"You get to hang out, take it easy," Reva continued. "I'm stuck in the stupid store practically every day, for the last two weeks."

Pam was silent at the other end. Reva chuckled to herself. My cousin is such a wimp, she thought. Why doesn't Pam ever speak up? Why doesn't she ever have the nerve to tell me what she's *really* thinking?

"I've got to get off, Reva," Pam said. "My dad wants to use the phone."

"You should get your own line," Reva said cruelly. "Anyway, my dad wanted me to invite you for Christmas Eve. As usual."

Reva stifled a yawn. Why does Dad insist on having them over every year? Doesn't he get tired of pretending we're all one big happy family?

She chatted a few minutes more with Pam, blowing on her nails, checking her hair in the mirror over her dressing table. Pam seems distant, Reva thought. Maybe she's decided to give up pretending we have anything in common.

Reva had heard that Pam had been hanging out with Mickey Wakely and Clay Parker, just about the worst kids at Shadyside High.

What was she trying to prove, anyway? Reva wondered. Doesn't she care about her reputation? Doesn't Pam even want to *pretend* that she has a chance to make something of her life?

After all, Reva thought, Pam didn't have it so bad. Sure, she didn't have a big house or good clothes. But at least she still had a mother, someone to talk to, someone to share things with.

Tenderly running a finger along her cut lip, Reva said goodbye to her cousin and, glancing at the clock, replaced the phone receiver. Feeling the nearly healed lip gave her a shiver of dread and, for a moment, she considered not going in to work. She was already half an hour late, after all.

But then she thought about Mitch and changed her mind.

Mitch, Mitch—what's your problem? she thought, feeling exasperated. It was more than two weeks since they'd started their vacation jobs at Dalby's. Two weeks of dropping Mitch subtle hints—and not-so-subtle hints. Still he hadn't made a move.

Was he so attached to that drippy Lissa that he was choosing to ignore the fact that Reva was coming on to him? Was he just impossibly shy?

Today's the day, Reva decided. I'll make the first move myself.

It's time for a very direct approach.

And then poor little Lissa can start searching for a new boyfriend, someone as wimpy and washed out as she is.

Reva pulled off the sweater she was wearing and changed into a white cashmere turtleneck. She knew it looked great on her. It really showed off her figure, and the soft white cashmere brought out her blue eyes and dramatic red hair.

After rearranging her curls, she grabbed her bag and started toward the door—and was surprised to see that she'd had an audience.

"Michael—what are you doing here?" she asked her little brother.

"I wanted to ask you something," he said, gripping the doorknob with both hands and leaning against the door.

"How long were you standing there?" Reva asked sharply. "You know you're supposed to knock."

Michael shrugged. "Will you take me to the store today?"

"What?" She tried to push past him into the hallway, but he moved quickly to block the door.

"Take me to the store. Please?"

"Why, Michael?"

"To see Santa Claus."

Reva suddenly remembered that she had promised to take him to see Santa. It had completely slipped her mind.

She gazed down at him. She could never get over the fact that he looked so much like her. "I can't today," she said softly, reaching out and affectionately playing with his curly red hair. "I'm late for work."

"Will you get fired?" he asked seriously.

Reva laughed. "No. I don't think Daddy will let them fire me," she told him.

"So why can't I come see Santa?" he insisted, still blocking the doorway.

"I'll take you, Michael," Reva assured him. "But not today."

"When?"

"Soon."

"When is soon?"

"Soon." She took his arm and pulled it aside so she could get by him. Then she hurried down to the front closet to get her coat.

Poor kid, she thought. He misses having a mom more than I do. I think he's really lonely.

Pulling on her coat, she vowed to spend more time with him. Then she stepped outside into a sunny but cold morning. The sudden cold made her sore lip throb.

It had to be Hank who did this to me, she thought angrily.

Who else could it have been?

Such a vicious trick.

Starting up the Volvo, she forced it out of her mind. She wanted to concentrate on Mitch.

"This is your day, Mitch," she said aloud, turning the car around in the circle at the end of the drive and heading down to the street.

He was so good-looking, with those adorable dimples on both cheeks when he smiled and that scratchy, hoarse little-boy voice. She liked his taste in clothes too—polo shirts, cuffed chinos—preppy without being *too* showy.

"This is your day, Mitch," she repeated, grinning.

She thought about him all the way to work.

She found him at lunchtime in the electronics department stockroom, unloading a crate of CD players. He was wearing a white sweatshirt and chinos.

"Hi," Reva said, walking up close behind him.

He jumped up, startled by her voice.

She laughed. He blushed.

"Hey—we match!" she exclaimed, pointing to their white sweaters. She deliberately stood very close to him.

"Yeah," he said, trying to back up. But he was already against the wall shelves. "How's it going, Reva? I've been unloading cartons all morning. We got in an entire truck of CDs and stereos."

"I've been thinking about you," Reva said, making her voice low and whispery. She opened her eyes wide and stared meaningfully into his, giving him her best smile, lips slightly parted.

"Oh, yeah?" He glanced down at the carton, still half-filled with boxes of CD players. "I have to finish unloading these," he said uncomfortably.

"It's lunchtime," Reva replied. "You can take a break. The boss's daughter gives you permission."

He laughed. "Thanks."

"I said I've been thinking about you," Reva repeated, staring into his eyes.

"I've been thinking about you too," he said in his scratchy voice, his words sounding hurried, as if he wanted to get them all out at once. "I think we should talk."

"I don't want to talk," Reva said, leaning forward. "I want to do this."

She reached out quickly and put her hands behind his head. Then she pulled his face to hers and pressed her lips against his.

He let out a small gurgle of surprise but kissed her back. She held him against her, pressing the back of his head with both hands.

Not a bad kisser, she thought.

Her eyes went up to the security camera. She realized that Hank might be watching this passionate scene.

Good, she thought, moving her lips against Mitch's, holding his head and moving her fingers through his hair. I hope you get an eyeful, Hank. I hope you enjoy the show.

She lowered her hands to Mitch's shoulders and kissed him with renewed passion.

Are you watching, Hank? Are you watching it all?

What's wrong with me? she suddenly thought. Why am I standing here kissing Mitch and thinking about Hank?

She held Mitch tightly, kissing him harder as if that might drive Hank from her mind.

"Whoa!" an angry voice cried from behind them.

Mitch pulled out of her grasp. Reva spun around to see who had the nerve to interrupt them.

"Lissa!" Mitch cried, his eyes wide, his open mouth smeared with Reva's magenta lipstick.

Chapter 11

FIRST BLOOD

"Oh, hi, Lissa," Reva said calmly. "What do *you* want?"

Lissa, her face crimson, her small hands tightened into fists, ignored Reva and stared only at Mitch.

"We're kind of busy right now," Reva told Lissa, pushing at her hair, straightening her white sweater. She reached out and wiped some of her lipstick off Mitch's chin.

Lissa, standing rigidly in the stockroom doorway, continued to stare at Mitch. Angry tears had formed in the corners of her eyes.

"Reva—" Lissa started, talking now through clenched teeth and shifting her attention to Reva. "You can't just play with people."

"Who's *playing?*" Reva cracked and laughed at her own line.

Mitch opened his mouth to say something to Lissa,

but then closed it and lowered his eyes to stare at his shoes.

Lissa cried out, more in disgust than anger, furious that Mitch hadn't the courage to say anything. Then she turned and fled from the room.

"Lissa—wait!" Mitch finally cried out.

"What a bore. Now, where were we?" Reva asked, turning her sexiest, most devilish smile on him.

But Mitch had pushed past her and taken off after Lissa. "Hey—wait! Lissa—wait!"

"Let her go!" Reva called after him.

Oh, brother, she thought, rolling her eyes. What is his *problem?*

But she chased after him, into the electronics department with its wall of color TVs, all tuned to Oprah Winfrey, fifty Oprah Winfreys staring at Reva as she grabbed Mitch by the arm and pulled him back.

"Let her go," Reva instructed him.

"I can't," he insisted heatedly, his eyes searching the wide aisle for Lissa. She had disappeared.

"Don't be a wimp," Reva said. The Oprah Winfreys grinned at her, speaking silently into a microphone, as if giving a play-by-play of what she and Mitch were doing.

"Hey—let go of me, Reva," Mitch said angrily.

She opened her eyes wide and pouted in a mock display of having her feelings hurt. "Come on, Mitch," she urged in her low, sexy voice. "Let's go back to the stockroom. We can talk about it there."

Mitch, still searching for Lissa, shook his head no.

Reva turned away from the smiling Oprah Winfreys

and saw Hank come around the corner from the freight elevators, heading toward her. Quickly she stepped closer to Mitch and draped her arm affectionately around his shoulder. She nuzzled against Mitch, who was momentarily too startled to react.

Does this make you jealous, Hank? Reva thought as Hank passed by, staring at her but not saying hello.

Does this make you jealous?

I hope so.

"Reva, please," Mitch said edgily, pulling away from her. "You know, what we were doing—I mean —back there—" He pointed toward the stockroom against the back wall. "Well, it wasn't right. I mean—"

"What *do* you mean?" Reva asked softly, patiently.

Mitch took a deep breath and started again. "Lissa and I have been going together a long time. And I just don't think it was fair to her—"

Reva reached out and rubbed more lipstick off his face. "I like you, Mitch," she said in her most kittenish voice. "You like me too—don't you?"

He blushed and swept his hand back through his straight, dark hair.

"You *seemed* to like me . . . back there," Reva said, glancing back to the stockroom.

"I just think—well—"

Poor Mitch, Reva thought, amused. He's totally flustered.

"Oh. Look at the time!" Reva cried suddenly, staring at her watch. "I promised I'd be back at my post ten minutes ago! Ms. Smith will *kill* me! She'll probably club me with her shoulder pads!" She rubbed his cheek with the back of her hand. "See you later."

Then, before Mitch had a chance to respond, she turned and ran, heading for the bank of elevators on the other side of the store, leaving him standing still with his mouth agape, just as the fifty Oprahs waved goodbye.

The store was crowded with lunchtime shoppers, office workers mostly, crowding around the costume jewelry counters, a few housewives pushing strollers, shopping bags draped over the handles.

That went better than I thought, Reva told herself, a pleased smile on her newly lipsticked lips. Having Lissa burst in on us like that was an added treat.

I'll never forget the horrified look on Mitch's face, she thought.

What a wimp.

But at least he'll be *my* wimp soon.

A line of five or six kids, dressed in snowsuits and wool caps, made Reva realize she was passing Santa Land at the front of the Dalby toy department. Sure enough, there was Robb up in Santa's big, red- and white-candy-striped throne, a scared-looking toddler on his lap.

As Reva passed by, the kid tilted his head back and then exploded a wet sneeze right in Robb's face.

Reva laughed out loud. What a riot!

Poor Robb will be wiping snot off his face for a week!

Reva was still chuckling when she reached the

perfume counter and took her place behind the display shelves. Ms. Smith stepped away from the cash register alcove and approached Reva, glancing angrily at her watch.

"I'm glad you find being late so amusing," she snapped.

"I wasn't smiling about that," Reva replied coldly.

"Well, you've made me fifteen minutes late for my luncheon engagement," Miss Smith accused.

"Terribly sorry," Reva told her, not sounding the least bit sorry.

"There are customers waiting," Reva's supervisor scolded, then grabbed up her bag and started off.

"Have a good lunch," Reva called with exaggerated sweetness.

Ms. Smith turned back. "There's a package for you," she told Reva. "That one there. With the gift wrapping. I don't know who left it. Open it when all the customers have gone."

Reva watched Ms. Smith hurry away through the crowded aisle. As soon as she was out of sight, Reva picked up the package and carried it to the cash register alcove, turning her back to the counter so that customers couldn't disturb her.

The package was square and was neatly wrapped in silver-foil wrapping paper with a red bow taped to the top.

How odd, Reva thought, turning the package over in her hands. Is this an early Christmas present from someone? Who would know to leave it here at the perfume counter? It must be some kind of surprise from Daddy, she decided.

"Miss! Miss?" a woman was calling loudly to Reva.

She ignored the customer and, being careful of her fingernails, tore open the package.

There was a box inside. Reva eagerly tore the top off the box and pulled out a dark, gracefully shaped bottle.

It was some sort of perfume or cologne.

Such an unusual bottle, Reva thought, admiring the smooth red glass, examining it curiously.

It's so heavy, it must be very expensive, she figured.

She carefully removed the glass stopper and started to raise it to her nose.

She stopped when she saw the drops of dark red liquid clinging to the bottom of the stopper.

Suddenly suspicious, Reva put the stopper down, then tilted the bottle onto her outstretched finger.

It's not cologne—it's *blood!*

Reva uttered a low cry.

The bottle slipped from her hand, hit the hard countertop, and shattered.

Two customers, women leaning on the other side of the counter, also cried out in alarm as blood from the bottle splashed over the front of Reva's white cashmere sweater.

Chapter 12

IS HANK GUILTY?

When Reva was five and attending a private kinder-garten in a luxury building in the hills overlooking the Conononka River, she had a run-in with another little girl that she never forgot.

The other little girl, Reva remembered, was a troublesome, willful blond girl named Sara. One day Reva and Sara were painting on easels, using large sheets of white paper and wide brushes that they dipped into open cans of paint.

An argument developed between Reva and Sara, a territorial dispute of some kind. Reva couldn't re-member which of them started it.

But it ended with Sara hoisting up the big can filled with red paint and pouring it over Reva's head.

The thick red paint ran down Reva's face, oozed down her sweater and white jeans. And somehow *in her mind* the paint, as it oozed and soaked into her clothing, became blood.

She was only five, after all, and had never been the victim of any kind of violent attack.

And standing helplessly, in a kind of shock, seeing —and feeling—the paint roll down her body, cover her skin and her clothes, Reva began to scream.

And scream.

And according to what her mother later told her, it took hours to get her to stop. Long after her clothes had been changed and the paint had been scrubbed away, Reva still begged her mother to "wash away the blood."

Twelve years later, standing behind the perfume counter as the blood splashed up onto her sweater, the violent scene in the kindergarten flashed vividly into Reva's mind.

But this time, after uttering a silent cry of surprise, of disgust, she didn't scream.

Other people were screaming.

Reva clamped her teeth shut as if trapping in all emotions, shutting away all feeling. She held her arms straight out, away from her sides, not wanting to touch her sweater, not wanting to touch the blood.

No, she thought.

No screams this time.

She clenched her teeth so hard it hurt and silently stared down at the oozing red mess.

No screams.

I don't feel it, she told herself, concentrating with all her strength.

I don't feel anything.

"I'm okay," she assured the horrified customers clustered at the counter. "Please—I'm okay."

She was still trying to reassure them, to quiet them, wondering how to get the mess cleaned up, wondering what to do about her ruined sweater, when she saw the small envelope, half covered in blood on the floor at her feet.

She bent over quickly and picked it up, surprised to realize that she was out of breath, gasping for air, her heart pounding in her chest.

It was a gift card. It must have fallen out of the package.

Reva ripped open the envelope with trembling, bloody fingers. A small white card tucked inside had a message printed on it in red ink: HAPPY HOLIDAYS FROM A FRIEND.

Some friend, Reva thought bitterly.

The same friend who hid the needle in my lipstick.

Some friend with a very sick sense of humor.

Hank.

Yeah. Probably Hank.

This is the kind of dumb juvenile thing that would really appeal to him.

His stupid way of paying me back.

What a dork! Reva thought, feeling the anger rise up from the pit of her stomach. What a total creep. Does he really think I'll be terrified because he pulls a couple of dumb jokes like this?

Does he think I'll go screaming hysterically out of the store and never return?

Does he think I'll be frightened out of my wits or something?

This just proves I was right about him, Reva decided. This just proves that he doesn't know me very well.

In fact, he doesn't know me at all.

Because I'm not going to scream and cry. No way.

What I'm going to do is go right upstairs and get him fired.

You're out of here, Hank, Reva thought, allowing a smile to cross her face. No more idiotically cruel jokes. You're out of here.

Ignoring the cries and worried conversations of the alarmed customers, Reva hurried from the booth, jogging quickly down the aisle, past staring, startled onlookers, to the employees' elevator.

She rode up to the sixth floor and stepped out into the reception area. "Hey, Reva—" the receptionist behind the wide oak desk called to her. But Reva was already halfway down the hall to her father's office in the corner.

She came to an abrupt halt in front of the tall bank of security monitors, surprised to see several blue-uniformed workers there. Somewhat to her relief, Hank wasn't at his post. The tall stool in front of the monitors was empty.

He's probably goofing off somewhere, Reva thought. Or maybe cooking up another joke to ruin more of my clothes.

But then she saw him, on his back on the floor behind the bank of monitors, attentively attaching several cable wires. The other workers were fitting what appeared to be VCRs into new shelves beside the monitors.

Hank looked up as she started to pass. "Reva?"

She glared angrily at him, her blue eyes clear and cold as ice, her teeth clenched. She wanted to accuse him. She wanted to scream at him. She wanted to let him know why she was on her way into her father's office.

She wanted to hit him and tear at his blond, spiky hair and make him hurt, make him hurt bad, for embarrassing her, for frightening her—for tricking her.

But she didn't want to make a scene in front of all of these workers.

Instead, she leaned over Hank, who was still on his back hooking up cables, and in a low voice said, "I know it was you."

He sat up with a start, his dark eyes wide with surprise. "Huh?"

"Don't act dumb," she said, forcing herself to keep her voice low and calm.

"What happened to you? You're a mess," he said innocently, his eyes narrowing with concern. "Are you okay?"

"You never were a very good actor," Reva insisted. "I know it was you, Hank. And it's going to cost you."

"Listen, Reva—I'm kind of busy here," Hank said impatiently, ignoring her threat, gesturing to the swarm of workers in the area. "We're installing a VCR for each monitor. We'll have everything the security cameras pick up on tape every day."

"Thrills and chills," Reva said sarcastically, rolling her eyes. The blood had soaked through her sweater to her skin. It felt wet and sticky and uncomfortable.

She studied his face, trying to decide if he was putting on the innocent act or if he really didn't know what she was talking about. Staring at him, she began to feel less certain.

"You're saying you didn't leave a package for me at my perfume counter?" Reva asked.

He shook his head. "I've been here since morning. Haven't even had lunch yet. Ask these guys." He gestured to the workers, who were fitting the last of the VCRs onto the shelves.

"You're lying!" she shouted.

Several of the workers turned to gape at her, startled by her bloody appearance and loud outburst.

"You're lying," she repeated, this time in a whisper.

"I heard you the first time," Hank said dryly.

"Look at my sweater!" she cried, feeling her anger rise again, feeling herself slipping out of control despite all of her attempts to hold herself together.

"Is that blood?" he asked, sliding out from under the console. "Or is it paint?"

"You know what it is!" she cried and, unwilling to let him see her out of control, fled. Past the other executive offices. Past the wide balcony that looked over the five floors below. Without stopping to see how bad the stain was, without stopping to try to wash it off, she ran to the end of the hall and her father's office.

You're out of here, Hank.

I don't care if you play dumb or not.

You're out of here. One word to my dad, and you're out of here.

And happy holidays to you too.

She caught a glimpse of herself in the mirror on the wall outside her father's office and gasped, seeing all of the blood-smeared sweater for the first time.

How could he *do* this to me? she wondered.

Mr. Dalby's office door was closed. Reva raised her hand to knock just as Josie, her father's secretary, came out. "Is my dad in there?" Reva asked breathlessly.

"Yes, but he's in a very important meeting," Josie told her. "I'm not allowed to interrupt him for anything."

"Oh." Reva sighed. She could feel her energy begin to drain. Her conversation with her father would have to wait. She knew better than to interrupt him while he was in an important meeting. "Guess I'll go home and change," she said.

Josie stared back at her, her eyes on the huge, dark stain. "You might be able to bleach that out. Is it paint?"

"No, it's blood, and it's ruined," Reva muttered.

She headed back to the elevator, walking slowly,

dispiritedly now. She had just passed the balcony when a terrifying sound—a deafening *pop-pop-pop*—shattered the air.

"Oh!" Reva cried out and froze in fear.

She knew that sound from TV.

The sound of machine guns.

اضطراری نمی آید این متن نامفهوم
Reva heard from the floors below

Chapter 13

SQUEALING TIRES

*R*eva heard screams from the floors below.

Fearing more gunfire, she dropped to her knees beside the low balcony wall.

Everything seemed to stop. All sound. All movement. Even her breathing seemed to stop as she waited, too terrified to look over the balcony railing.

She was still on her knees, still holding her breath, when the door to her father's office burst open. Mr. Dalby bounded through the door in his shirtsleeves, his face red, his eyes wide with fear.

"What was that noise?" he called out. "Was that gunfire?"

Reva climbed quickly to her feet. "Daddy—"

She didn't get another word out. Mr. Dalby had fixed his eyes on Reva's blood-splattered sweater. He gaped in horror. "Reva—you're *shot!*" he managed to cry. Then his eyes rolled up in his head, and he uttered a low moan and slumped to the floor.

"Daddy—!" Reva repeated, overcoming her fear and rushing toward him.

Josie got to him first, dropped to her knees, lifted his wrist to find a pulse. "Help—somebody!" she cried. "Get help!"

Reva dropped down on the other side of her father, her heart pounding. She felt helpless and frantic.

Silenced footsteps hurried across the carpet. People were running out of offices, making hushed phone calls, huddling over her father.

"Daddy?" Reva grabbed his hand. "Is he okay? Is he breathing?" she asked Josie.

Mr. Dalby stirred. He opened his eyes and fixed them on Reva, his expression dazed, confused.

"Daddy—?" She squeezed his hand.

"Are you okay?" he asked. "Were you—shot?"

"No, I'm fine," Reva said, squeezing his hand. "I'm okay. Really. I'm okay."

Mr. Dalby sat up and rubbed the back of his head. "Ouch. Did I faint or something?"

Josie nodded her head.

"It was the blood," Reva's father said. "First I heard the gunfire. Then I saw Reva—"

"I—uh—I spilled something," Reva explained, deciding not to tell the truth, deciding that her father had had enough of an upset for one day.

He stood up shakily, holding on to Reva's shoulder for support. His face, which had gone as white as cake flour when he fainted, began to get its color back. He ran a hand back through his graying hair.

Suddenly a blue-uniformed store worker pushed his way through the crowd of onlookers. "Mr. Dalby, that sound you heard—"

"Yes?" Mr. Dalby, his strength seemingly restored, released Reva's shoulder and stepped eagerly toward the man.

"It was the Christmas tree lights," the man reported nervously.

"What?"

"A power surge, sir. A string of lights shorted out," the worker explained. "I guess it started a chain reaction. The lights started to pop, dozens of them all at once. Then the whole thing just shorted out."

Mr. Dalby, obviously somewhat relieved, took a deep breath, then blew the air silently out through his mouth. "These electrical problems are driving me nuts," he said, shaking his head. "Is this power surge connected to the other problems we've been having?"

"Probably, sir," the worker replied, shifting his weight uncomfortably. "We're not sure."

"Any idea what caused the power surge?"

"We're checking," came the reply.

"Let's all get back to work," Mr. Dalby told the crowd of onlookers. "I'm okay. Everything seems to be okay." He told the worker to get the tree lights back on as soon as possible, then started back to his office, rubbing the back of his head.

Reva followed him to the door. "You sure you're okay?" she asked.

"You gave me a real scare," he said, suddenly looking very old. "What on earth did you spill on your sweater?"

She was tempted to tell him but held herself back. "I'll tell you later," she said.

"You came up to see me?" he asked, glancing at his watch.

"I—I just wanted to tell you I was going home to change," Reva replied.

"Why don't you just pick out a new sweater here in the store?" he suggested.

She laughed. "Shop in *this* tacky store?" she asked with exaggerated horror. "Please, Daddy! Give me credit for better taste than that!"

He chuckled, kissed her on the forehead, and headed back into his office to resume his meeting.

Always leave 'em laughing, Reva told herself as she waved goodbye to Josie, who was back on the phone, and headed past the low balcony, past the bank of security monitors without even looking to see if Hank was still there, to the employees' elevator. She was eager to get her coat and go on home.

The afternoon sun was high in a cloudless sky. The air was brisk but not uncomfortably cold. Reva started up the Volvo, then sat listening to the steady hum of the engine for a short while before pulling out of the employee parking lot.

"What a day," she said out loud.

She snapped on the radio, listened to a few seconds of a loud commercial, then snapped it off again.

The silence felt good. She turned the corner, shielding her eyes from the sudden burst of sunlight that spread over the windshield.

She thought about Mitch. About kissing Mitch. About kissing him hard and long.

She pictured Lissa bursting in again, catching them. The expression on poor Lissa's face.

Everything was worth it just for that one look of horror, that one look of . . . defeat.

Too bad Mitch was such a wimp.

But, Reva thought, I can amuse myself with him for the time being.

Her thoughts had turned to Hank and to the cologne bottle filled with blood when she noticed the car behind her. It was a white Taurus.

Had it been right behind her the whole way home? Staring at it in the rearview mirror, Reva felt a sudden stab of fear.

She made a quick right turn onto a narrow street she'd never been on before. Small, close-together clapboard houses lined both sides of it.

That white Taurus, she thought. It didn't turn too—did it?

One glance in the mirror told her that it had.

I'm being followed, she realized. This isn't possible. This doesn't happen in real life, does it? This only happens on TV shows.

Her heart pounding, she sped up, then made a quick left turn without signaling.

Reluctantly she checked the mirror, hoping that the car wouldn't be there. But it was still there and close behind.

"Go away. Please! Go away!"

Reva roared through a stop sign, studying the mirror, trying to see the driver. But the bright sunlight formed a curtain over the Taurus's windshield.

She made a right and found herself back on a crowded main road. The Taurus, she saw, was staying close behind.

This isn't happening. It isn't.

Who can it be?

She caught a glimpse of a man's face, a dark mustache, a cap pulled down over his eyes.

What does he want?

She immediately thought of kidnapping. Sometimes, she knew, the children of very wealthy people were kidnapped and held for huge ransoms.

He'll drag me to some abandoned house and tie me up. And if my dad won't pay, he'll kill me and leave me there.

No!

She floored the gas pedal.

And made a decision.

She'd be safer at home. She'd pull right up the drive, into the garage, and run into the house through the garage entrance.

That was her best chance.

Struggling to calm her breathing, struggling to hold back her terrified thoughts, Reva made another sharp turn and headed for home.

The white Taurus squealed around the corner and followed, only a car length behind.

"What do you want? What do you *want?*" Reva

screamed over the roar of the car engine. She swerved around a school bus. A horn honked loudly. The Taurus kept the pace.

Did this guy send the bottle of blood? The thought flashed into her mind, sending fresh fear down her spine.

Is it possible that it wasn't Hank? That whoever's following me sent the blood and put the needle in my lipstick?

But why?

As a warning?

As a warning that even worse things were in store?

She sighed out loud as she turned into her driveway. A few more seconds and she'd be in back of the house, in the safety of the garage. A few more seconds and she'd be inside the kitchen. She could call the police and—

The Taurus pulled into the drive right behind her.

"I don't believe this!"

Reva hit the brakes hard. She'd forgotten her garage door opener, and the garage door was closed!

The Volvo slid to a halt. The Taurus squealed over the asphalt drive, stopping inches behind her.

I'm trapped now, Reva thought. I can't get into the garage. But I can't just sit here in the car.

Her only hope, she decided, was to make a run for the house.

If she could get to it and get inside . . .

She grabbed her house key, flung open the car door and, breathing heavily, leapt out of the car and started running around it toward the house.

Her legs felt heavy, as if they were weighted down. Her chest felt ready to explode.

Glancing to the drive, she saw that the man in the cap was out of his car. He was big and tough looking and was running after her.

Chapter 14

LOSING IT

"Hey—" he called, stumbling after her.

Reva was almost to the door.

"Hey—" The man was waving wildly to her.

She pulled open the glass storm door, jammed her key in the lock, and pushed hard.

It didn't budge.

Wrong key.

"Hey—" He was only a few yards behind now.

Reva spun around to face him, her mouth open, about to scream, her features stretched wide.

Breathing hard, her pursuer stopped at the bottom of the stoop. "Your taillight—it's broken," he said between gulps of air.

"What?" Reva remained frozen in place, her back pressed against the glass storm door.

"Your taillight. I accidentally bumped into it back

in Dalby's parking lot," the man said, struggling to regain his breath.

Reva stared at him, not understanding, still waiting for him to make his move, to spring his plan of terror on her.

"I accidentally smashed into your taillight. I'm really sorry," the man said, taking off his cap and wiping perspiration off his broad forehead. "Come here. I'll show you."

He started back toward her car.

"My taillight?" Reva cried, not recognizing her own terror-tight voice. "You followed me all the way here because of my taillight?"

Still feeling shaky and uncertain, she followed him back to the driveway. Sure enough, her left taillight was exposed, the plastic over the bulb knocked off and gone.

"I hate it when people bump your car and then just drive off," the man explained, replacing his cap. "So I followed you. I was trying to signal you. Didn't you see me?"

"Uh . . . no," Reva replied, feeling very foolish.

"Here." The man shoved a small white card into her hand. "That's my insurance agent. Let me write my name and number on the other side. The insurance company will take care of everything. I'm sorry about it. Just careless, I guess."

Reva's hand was still trembling as she took the card from the man. She felt weak, totally drained.

How could I have let myself get so scared over nothing? she asked herself.

She thanked the man for being so thoughtful.

What a waste of time, she thought. Daddy'll just have the car fixed at his garage. Why bother involving an insurance company over a stupid taillight?

"Thanks again!" she called as the man climbed into his car and backed down the long drive.

I'm losing it. I'm really losing it, Reva thought, slowly making her way up to the house.

This man was being a good citizen, and I acted like a paranoid nut-case!

Oh, well, she told herself, unlocking the kitchen door and calling out "hello." Her call hung unanswered in the silent house, and she knew Yvonne and Michael must be out. I do have reason to be paranoid, though.

She tossed her coat down and pulled off the blood-soaked sweater.

Whoever's trying to scare me is doing a really good job, Reva decided.

First my cut lip. Then the hideous bottle of blood.

She opened the cabinet under the sink and shoved the sweater into the wastebasket.

What's next? she wondered with a cold shudder.

What's next?

PART TWO

SILENT NIGHTS

Chapter 15

NOTHING TO BE NERVOUS ABOUT

"*I*'m so nervous, I can hardly breathe," Pam said.

"Nothing to be nervous about," Clay said, slumped down in the passenger seat beside her, his knees on the dashboard, his eyes focused straight ahead on the red taillights of the traffic outside the window.

"You talked to Maywood today?" Mickey asked from the backseat, clearing his throat, his voice sounding choked and scared.

"No. Not today," Clay replied tensely. "But I *told* you, it's all worked out. Every detail. We lucked out too—the new video security system hasn't been hooked up yet. They were using some kid to set it up, and he blew it."

The big Pontiac rolled to a stop at a traffic light. The front seat was suddenly flooded with light from a street lamp above the intersection.

Pam glanced over at Clay, who was dressed in black denims and a black turtleneck. No coat despite the temperature in the twenties outside.

"We want to be able to move fast," he had explained as they were preparing for the robbery, going over the plan one last time in Mickey's living room. "Got to stay light, stay agile." Clay smiled as he talked.

He really isn't nervous, Pam had realized, struggling to tie her sneakers with trembling hands. He's excited, terribly excited. He's . . . eager.

She wished she could have Clay's confidence.

No. She wished she had never agreed to be in on this robbery in the first place. It was too frightening. Too dangerous.

Sure, Clay told them repeatedly that it wasn't a real robbery. That there was no danger. No risk. No chance of a slipup.

But how reliable was Clay?

Going over the plan in Mickey's living room, Pam had wanted to disappear. Run away. Move into someone else's life till this was all over.

"Don't you have a darker sweater than that?" Clay complained, taking in the butter-colored pullover Mickey was wearing.

"I'll check," Mickey said, hurrying to his room. He returned a few minutes later in a black T-shirt.

Mr. Wakely was out. They had the house to themselves.

"I feel sick," Pam told Clay. "Really. I do."

His expression hardened. "You just have to drive," he had said, his steel-gray eyes narrowing as he studied her face.

Now, here they were, half an hour later, a little past eleven-thirty on a Friday night, driving to Dalby's.

The light changed to green. Pam pushed down on the gas, and the big, old Pontiac rumbled forward.

"Wow, man, not many cars on the road for a Friday night," Mickey said quietly from the backseat.

"We don't need a traffic report," Clay snapped.

"I really feel sick," Pam said. "My whole body is shaking."

"Maybe you should pull over till you feel better," Mickey suggested.

"Just drive," Clay insisted. "Concentrate on driving and you won't feel sick."

"Thanks, Doc," Pam said sarcastically.

Clay groaned, plainly annoyed at both of them. "Are you two wimps going to be any help or not?"

"Come on, man. Chill," Mickey said, reaching up to the front seat to pat Clay on the shoulder. "We're fine. We're all fine, aren't we, Pam?"

A police black-and-white pulled up behind them.

"Slow down!" Clay shouted to Pam, ducking low in the seat.

"I'm only going thirty-five," Pam said, staring into the rearview mirror.

The police car seemed to hesitate for a moment on their tail, then passed them on the left and sped on ahead.

All three of them burst out laughing as the black-and-white moved out of sight. Nervous, relieved laughter.

"Did my hair turn white?" Pam asked.

"You were cool," Mickey congratulated her, flopping back against his seat. "Man, you were cool."

"Now, remember, we go to electronics first," Clay said, turning around in the seat to talk to Mickey.

"I remember," Mickey told him. "We go to electronics first because it's farthest from the back door. We go to the farthest place first, then work our way back to the door."

"Right. Score one for Mickey," Clay said dryly.

"I want to get one of those bomber jackets," Mickey said with enthusiasm. "You know, the leather ones with the neat patches?"

"Yeah. Get one for me too," Pam said. Then, without warning, she hit the brakes, pulling the car to the curb across from an empty lot.

"Hey—" Clay cried angrily. "What are you doing?"

"I can't do this," Pam said, gripping the steering wheel tightly with both hands, staring straight ahead through the dark windshield.

"Come on, Pam," Clay said, softening his tone a little, turning to face her. "You just have to drive—remember?"

"That's right," Mickey chimed in, leaning forward. "You just sit in the car and wait for us, Pam. That's all."

He stared at Clay as if seeking Clay's approval for

what he had just said. But Clay was concentrating all his attention on Pam.

"I don't think I can do that," Pam said, not meeting either of their eyes. Her hands began to ache. She loosened her grip on the wheel. "I don't think I can just sit there and wait. I'll go crazy. I won't be able to take it."

"Well, what do you want?" Clay asked, unable to hide his impatience. "You want to come in with us?"

Pam considered it for a long moment. "Yeah," she finally answered. "Yeah. I guess so." She turned to Clay. "I'll go in with you—but I won't take anything."

"Huh?"

"I'll go in with you. I think I'd be less nervous that way. But I won't take anything. I'll just wait inside for you two."

"Okay. Swell." Clay settled back in the seat. "If it'll make you feel better."

"That way, if something goes wrong," Pam conjectured, "I won't be sitting in the car all night, worried sick, wondering what happened."

"Nothing will go wrong," Clay said sharply. "How many times have I got to tell you?"

Pam took her foot off the brake, and the big car started to roll forward again. To her surprise, she realized that Dalby's was only a few blocks away.

"The plan. Go over it once again," she said, her throat tightening, her entire body going cold. "You know. Since it's different now."

Clay sighed noisily, acting out his exasperation.

He really is treating Mickey and me horribly, Pam thought. After all, it's not like any of us are hardened criminals. It's only natural that we're scared.

Maybe being angry at us is Clay's way of working off *his* nervousness, she decided.

"Look. The plan is exactly the same, even if you come into the store," Clay said, exasperated. "There are three loading docks in the back of the store. We drive past the first two and park the car in front of the third one. We leave the trunk down but unlatched. Maywood said he'd have the loading dock door open for us after eleven o'clock. We go in through that door, through the receiving room, along the employees' hall that leads to the main floor. We walk past all the perfume and cosmetics counters to the front of the first floor. Up a few steps, then down a few steps and into the electronics department."

"And Maywood is meeting us there?" Mickey asked.

"Yeah. He's meeting us there. He'll help us carry some stuff. We take what we want. We get it back to the loading dock and shove it into the trunk. Then we tie Maywood up and make it look like we overpowered him or something. Then we drive slowly and safely to my place."

"And stash the stuff in your garage," Mickey finished the plan for him.

Clay nodded. "No sweat. No big deal."

Pam turned sharply into the empty Dalby's parking lot. The glass-and-steel store loomed up ahead of them, brightly lighted with red and green Christmas lights streaming six stories down, as if the entire store had been gift wrapped.

"Do you hear me?" Clay was saying.

Pam realized that he'd been talking to her, telling her something. Her fear had drowned out his words.

"Pull around there," he instructed, pointing. "Not too fast. We don't want to draw attention from any cars on the street."

Feeling numb all over, feeling as if someone else were driving the car, someone else were turning the wheel, someone else were guiding them through the empty lot and around to the back, Pam followed Clay's instructions.

They rolled silently past the first concrete loading dock. Then past the second. It was dark back there, except for solitary, dim yellow lights, one over every door.

Pam pulled the car up even with the third loading dock, shifted into Park, and turned off the ignition. She peered out into the darkness. It was like being on the moon, she decided. The empty, silent employees' parking lot just beyond them, the darkened truck garage to her left.

So dark and empty.

It made her feel a little better.

Who could ever find them back here on the moon?

For some reason, her mom and dad flashed into her mind. They were home, watching some TV Christmas special when Pam had gone out. She'd told them she was going to the movies with some friends.

Some movie.

They were good parents, she decided. They were good to her. Proud of her. They even approved of Foxy.

She reached for the door handle and thought about Foxy.

Foxy would never believe she was doing this.

He was such a nice person, such a kind person. It would be hard for Foxy to understand how you can hate a person so much that you'd even rob to get back at them. That you could hate being poor so much—especially when the rest of your family was so rich.

She had wanted to tell Foxy about the robbery. She had even started to tell him a few nights before, but she stopped herself in time.

He wouldn't understand.

Pam wasn't sure that *she* understood.

Taking a deep breath, she pushed the car door open and stepped out into the cold.

"The lights," Clay whispered loudly, tapping the car's broad hood to get her attention. "Cut the lights."

It took Pam a while to realize she had forgotten to switch off the headlights. She reached back into the car, her hand fumbling over the dashboard until she pushed the right button.

It immediately grew much darker. Her two companions appeared as black shadows on black.

Pam unlatched the trunk, making sure the lid stayed down. Her hand was shaking as she struggled to shove the keys into her jeans pocket.

Then she followed the boys up the shallow concrete steps to the loading dock.

As they stepped into the faint glow from the small yellow bulb above the loading dock door, their breath smoking up above their heads, Pam hesitated.

Would the door be unlocked as promised?

And then she saw it—something gleamed in Clay's right hand.

"Clay—" she whispered, even though there was no one around.

He had one hand on the door, ready to turn the knob.

"Clay!" she called a little louder, not sure he had heard her.

He turned around as she moved past Mickey, who was shivering in his thin black T-shirt.

"Clay, what's that?" Pam asked.

Clay raised his right hand to reveal a small automatic pistol.

"Hey, man—" Mickey cried, staring stonily at his friend. "You didn't say anything about a gun."

"Come on, Clay—what do we need that for?" Pam asked, her eyes fixed on the small pistol, unable to conceal her horror.

"You never know," Clay said softly. He started to pull open the door.

121

Chapter 16

THIS WASN'T
SUPPOSED TO HAPPEN

*T*he door opened easily and they each slipped into the dark receiving area.

Silence.

It's so quiet, Pam thought, I can hear the boys breathing. I can practically hear them *thinking!*

Her eyes adjusted quickly to the dark. The receiving area, she could see, was just a long, empty space with a concrete floor, the place where cartons were stacked when they came off the trucks.

She crept up beside Clay, who stood stiffly, the pistol down at his side. "Didn't Maywood say he'd meet us here?" she whispered.

Clay shook his head. "No, he said he'd leave the door unlocked. He'll meet us in electronics." He pulled her arm gently. "Come on. Let's move."

"I wish you'd put that gun away," she whispered, following him.

He pretended not to hear her and continued walking quickly, taking long strides across the wide, empty area to the corridor. Pam hurried to keep up with him, glancing nervously back at Mickey, who lagged behind.

They reached the narrow hallway, which was also dark. The hallway was used by store employees only. It led to the employees' lounge, the stockrooms and, beyond those, the main selling floor.

"Hey—wait up!" Mickey called in a loud whisper.

"This way," Clay instructed, starting a slow jog down the corridor despite Mickey's plea.

He stopped at the edge of the main floor. Several ceiling lights had been left on. The store was about half as bright as normal.

Pam took a deep breath. The fragrances of a dozen different perfumes floated through the air. The store at night smelled sweet and stale at the same time. Across the vast room, the huge Christmas tree loomed, a towering, dark shape that rose up past the first of five balconies.

Silence.

All three of them stood at the entranceway, their eyes ranging over the width of the store. Nothing moved. No sign of anyone.

"The whole store is ours!" Mickey proclaimed jubilantly. "Wow!"

Clay turned back to him angrily. "Don't celebrate yet." He held the pistol at his waist.

"But this is *neat!*" Mickey exclaimed.

Pam wished she could feel as excited. Her mouth felt dry, her throat tight. She expected someone to jump out at them at any moment.

It's stifling in here, she thought, unzipping her coat. They turn off the air at night. We're breathing this afternoon's air. Leftover air. We're going to suffocate.

I can't breathe!

She scolded herself for starting to panic.

It's too late for that. You've come too far to panic now.

Taking a deep breath, and then another, she followed Clay and Mickey through the aisles of perfume and makeup counters, their sneakers squeaking softly on the hard floors.

Silence.

The silence is *thick,* Pam thought. I can *feel* it.

Strange thoughts. But who could blame her?

She stared up at the dark Christmas tree, then to the side of it to the balconies that overlooked them. Was someone standing on one of those balconies? Was there a security guard somewhere up there watching them make their way through the store?

No. Of course not.

Maywood would have thought of that. Wouldn't he?

Clay's voice interrupted her thoughts. "Up the stairs," he whispered, pointing with the pistol. "We go past Santa Land up there, then down another set of stairs, and we're in electronics."

"Wow," Mickey whispered, just behind Pam.

Someone was standing at the foot of the stairs.

Pam gasped and held back, grabbing on to a glass counter, ready to back away, to run.

But after a second of breath-stopping fright, she realized it wasn't a person, but a mannequin.

Behind her, Mickey let out a high-pitched giggle. He must have been frightened by the same mannequin.

They hurried up the low stairway, crossed the Santa area with its fake snow, its wooden, toy-laden sleigh complete with a single stuffed reindeer, and a tall, jutting barber pole, labeled NORTH POLE. Then down another low stairway into the large electronics department.

"We don't need Santa Claus, man!" Mickey exclaimed, rushing ahead of Pam and Clay, picking up the first VCR he found.

Clay scowled. He and Pam approached more cautiously. Pam's eyes searched the area, from the wall of TVs on one side, past the CDs and stereos to the cordless telephones and video game players on the other.

No one there.

Silence.

The only sound was the crackling of a faulty ceiling light above her head.

"Where's Maywood?" Pam whispered nervously, grasping Clay's sleeve.

He shrugged. "We can't stand around and wait for him," he said, his gray eyes hard and steady. "Let's get busy here."

Mickey had already picked up two cartons from behind a display shelf. "Hey, Clay—" he called. "What do I do with these VCRs?"

Clay uttered a low cry and slapped his own forehead. "I'm an idiot," he said. "We should've brought big bags or something to carry stuff in. Why didn't I think of it?"

The boys were talking too loudly, Pam thought, feeling her muscles tighten. Every sound they made frightened her more. She felt as if she were wearing her nerves outside her body.

The crackling of the overhead light was driving her crazy.

Mickey and Clay seemed to have forgotten about her entirely. They were huddled together, trying to solve the problem of how to carry the stuff they stole. Clay kept cursing himself out, telling himself how stupid he was for messing up this detail in the plan.

"Hey, I know, man. Maybe we can make several trips," Mickey suggested, still holding the two VCR cartons.

"Yeah. Of course," Clay replied, somewhat cheered. "We're in no hurry, right? We've got all the time in the world. We can take all night. Make as many trips as we want."

"Yeah!" Mickey agreed happily.

"Okay. Let's pile up the stuff," Clay said with renewed enthusiasm. "As much as we can fit into Pam's car."

Pam looked behind her, searched the long aisles, then stared back at the wall of TVs, dark and silent.

I should be home watching TV, she thought.

Home safe and sound with my parents. Watching the Grinch or something.

"Oh!" she cried out as she heard a sound.

Clay and Mickey froze in the aisle in front of her, staring back at her.

"Did you hear that?" Pam cried. She turned toward the sound. It seemed to have come from a small office to the right of the TVs.

"Hear what?" Clay asked, irritated.

"A noise. Like somebody dropped something," Pam managed to say, still staring at the office.

"I didn't hear anything," Mickey said.

"But it was *loud!*" she insisted.

Clay, the pistol raised, followed the direction of her gaze. "It came from over there?"

"That office," she said, holding on tightly to a countertop.

All three of them listened.

Silence now.

"That office is completely dark," Clay said, eyeing her suspiciously.

"So?" she cried.

"So don't scare us again," he warned coldly.

"Listen—I didn't make it up," Pam insisted.

"If you're not going to help, at least don't mess us up," Clay told her, pulling out a carton of Walkmans.

"Well, can't you hurry it up?" Pam asked anxiously, her voice so high-pitched she didn't recognize it.

Clay didn't reply. He only glared.

She glanced back at the office. It was completely

dark as Clay had said. She listened hard but heard only Mickey and Clay, pulling out CD players, and the annoying crackling of the ceiling light.

When she turned back to her two companions, she saw the blue-uniformed security guard.

He was very tall and tremendously overweight, Pam saw, with a beer belly hanging over his uniform pants. He was walking slowly, cautiously up the aisle behind Clay and Mickey. He had one hand resting on top of his gun holster.

Pam opened her mouth to warn her companions, but no sound came out.

She could only point.

Her fear began to ebb when she realized the intruder must be Maywood.

The guard stopped a few display cases behind Clay and Mickey. Despite his size, he had a baby face with big blue eyes and a stub of a nose. "Hello, folks!" he yelled cheerily. "Can I help you select anything?"

Both boys cried out in surprise and spun around. Mickey dropped the carton he was holding. It hit the floor at his feet with a loud crash.

"Hey—" Clay's mouth dropped open.

Why does Clay look confused? Pam wondered, her fear beginning to mount again.

"You're not Maywood!" Clay exclaimed. "Where's Maywood?"

The guard's expression turned hard. "Don't move. Don't talk," he warned.

"But Maywood—" Clay started.

"I *mean* it!" the guard bellowed, his large belly rising up as he screamed. "Any talking, I'll do it, hear?"

Mickey, all the color drained from his face, stared in disbelief at Clay. Pam, still leaning against the display case, felt her legs go weak. Her throat tightened.

I can't breathe, she thought.

I'm too frightened to breathe.

This wasn't supposed to happen. Clay *promised* us nothing would go wrong.

"Put your hands in the air," the guard instructed, one hand gesturing, the other still on top of his holster. "Put them high above your heads and keep them there."

Obediently raising her hands, Pam saw Mickey do the same. But Clay hesitated.

"Listen—" he called to the guard.

"Raise 'em!" the guard bellowed. "Now!"

Staring hard into the guard's unblinking eyes, Clay made no move to raise his hands.

"Maywood told us—" Clay started.

"Raise 'em!" the guard insisted. "Save your stories for the police." Without warning he lumbered forward quickly, leaned down, and pressed a button hidden under a display counter. A deafening alarm bell blared through the store.

"Run!" Clay shouted.

Without thinking, Pam started to run up the aisle, running blindly and breathlessly, the displays and mannequins a dim blur beside her.

She could hear Mickey a few yards behind her, hear his sneakers squeaking rapidly over the floor.

She could hear the guard yelling, calling to them.

At the low steps she turned and looked back.

And saw Clay facing the guard, his pistol raised.

"Clay—no!" Pam cried.

No, please no! she pleaded silently.

The guard, his baby face wide-eyed, startled, pulled his gun from its holster.

A gunshot.

The sound cut right through Pam.

She pressed her open hands over her face, afraid to look, afraid to cry out. Afraid to stay. Afraid to run.

"Clay—no!" Mickey shrieked from right beside her.

Pam watched the guard go down, clutching his bloodied chest, falling like a heavy sack of flour.

And now Clay, still holding the pistol, his face twisted in horror, was running, running to catch up with Pam and Mickey.

The alarm roared in her ears. It seemed to get louder, louder, until it felt as if it were coming from inside her head, and she thought her head would explode, explode from the sound, from what she had just seen.

And then the silence would return.

The cool, soft silence.

But, no. Clay caught up to them, pushed them both, forced them to start moving again. Up the low steps. Past the North Pole. Past Santa's gilded throne.

Goodbye, Santa Land.

Goodbye, Christmas.

Goodbye, childhood. Forever.

We're criminals now.

Clay shot the guard.

And now we're running, running, running.

Pam couldn't control her thoughts. Everything was out of control now.

They pounded over the floor. Through the aisles of sweet-smelling perfumes, past the smartly dressed mannequins.

Goodbye.

Goodbye to everything sweet smelling and good.

And still the alarm shrieked, following them, staying with them, behind them, ahead of them as they ran.

Through the narrow employees' corridor. Then through the empty darkness of the receiving area.

The siren surrounded them, captured them, held them.

Pam saw the gray door up ahead. The door that led out and away. The door that led to the dark, cool night.

The silent night.

She reached it first, pushed hard, and the door swung open.

Out onto the loading dock, the cold air rushing at her face. Mickey and Clay were right behind, gasping mouthfuls, their chests heaving as they struggled to breathe.

And still the roaring siren followed her. Even louder out there.

Got to get away. Got to drive away.

Got to *go!*

"Hey—" Mickey saw it first.

Then Pam.

"My car!" she cried. "It's gone!"

Chapter 17

MURDER

*T*rapped.

Who could have taken the car?

No time to think about it.

Over the maddening wail of the alarm, Pam could hear the rise and fall of other sirens. Police sirens. Growing louder.

Coming closer.

"We've got to get *out* of here!" she cried.

And then she saw the car.

It was right where she'd parked it at the loading dock to their right.

"We came out the wrong door!" Clay realized.

They had burst out onto the middle loading dock. Now, without hesitating, Pam jumped down, landing hard on the asphalt drive, and hurtled toward the car.

As she ran, Pam pulled the keys from her coat pocket. All three of them reached the car at the same time, their breath puffing above them, steamy and white against the night sky, the sirens wailing.

Clay slammed his fist on the trunk top, latching it.

It's empty, Pam found herself thinking.

All that fear. All that worry. All that . . . blood.

And the trunk is empty.

Pam slid behind the wheel and slammed the door shut. The sirens followed her inside the car. Clay and Mickey piled in, resuming their places.

The car sputtered, then started on the second try. Pam floored the gas pedal, and the big car squealed away, through the empty employees' parking lot, lurching over traffic bumps, then back onto Division Street, through a yellow light about to turn to red, and away.

Away, away, away.

Two police black-and-whites, their sirens crying out, passed them going the other way.

In the rearview mirror Pam watched them turn and pull into Dalby's parking lot.

In a few minutes they would find the guard. Lying in his own blood.

And then . . . what?

The dark stores gave way to dark houses. The streets whirled by silently.

Silent, at last. Silent again.

None of them spoke.

What was there to say?

Somehow Pam drove them home. Somehow Pam drove herself home.

* * *

The next morning she woke up in her clothes, the bed sheets and blankets in a tangled heap on the floor beside the bed.

It was all a dream, she told herself.

What a nightmare!

But then, why was she still dressed in the same clothes as in the dream? And why had she slept so fitfully?

And why was the dream so fresh, so vivid, so real in her mind?

Because, Pam knew, it wasn't a dream.

It had all really happened.

Yawning and rubbing her eyes, she bent to pull the bedclothes up off the floor, then glanced at the clock. Nine forty-five. Saturday morning.

She stood up, stretched, thought about changing into a fresh outfit, then decided against it.

How could she face her parents this morning?

She had the feeling that they would know. That they would know everything that had happened just by looking at her, by peering into her eyes.

She thought of Foxy. He would know too.

Everyone would know.

Her life was ruined.

She slumped into the bathroom, brushed her hair and her teeth. Then, feeling as if she hadn't slept, still hearing the insistent wail of the store alarm in the back of her mind, she descended the stairs and walked into the kitchen to face her parents.

The radio droned low in the background. Breakfast dishes were still on the table, but her parents were nowhere to be seen. At her usual place at the table Pam found a hastily scribbled note in her mother's handwriting.

The note read: "Your father still insists on paneling the den. I've gone with him to the lumber store so he doesn't pick anything too ghastly. Back soon. Love."

Pam felt relieved and disappointed at the same time. She didn't want to face her mom and dad this morning, but she didn't feel like being alone, either.

There were cereal boxes on the table, but Pam knew she couldn't eat anything. Her mouth felt dry as cotton. She poured herself a glass of orange juice and drank it down, pulp and all.

She was about to go back up to her room when the voice on the radio caught her attention. "A break-in at Dalby's Department Store on Division Street last night," Pam heard. She lunged for the radio, banging her knee against the counter, and turned up the volume.

"Ed Javors, a veteran security guard, was fatally shot," the announcer reported. "The burglars got away with twenty-five thousand dollars from a main-floor office safe. Shadyside police have assigned four men to the case. I'll have today's tri-city weather forecast in a moment."

Her forehead throbbing, Pam clicked off the radio. Her head lowered, she stood grasping the counter, trying to catch her breath.

Fatally shot.

The guard was fatally shot.

Killed.

And $25,000 in cash taken from a main-floor office safe.

This is *impossible,* Pam thought.

This didn't happen.

The guard was killed and $25,000 was stolen.

But how could that be?

She pushed herself away from the counter, slumped onto the chair at the table, and buried her head in her hands.

Got to think. Got to think. Got to think about this clearly.

But her thoughts spun wildly, whirling, whirling to the wail of the alarm siren.

Clay is a murderer.

He killed the guard. I saw him. I saw him shoot the guard.

And then—

No!

We didn't open the safe. We didn't take any money. We didn't take *anything!*

This story is wrong. All wrong. It *has* to be wrong.

Without realizing what she was doing, she had gotten up, walked over to the wall phone by the kitchen door, and was punching in Clay's number.

He picked up after the first ring.

"Clay—" Pam said. "Did you hear the radio?"

"Yeah," came the reply. His voice sounded hoarse, weary.

"It's wrong. It's all wrong!" Pam shrieked, unable to contain her panic.

"Tell me about it," Clay said quietly. "My gun wasn't loaded."

"Huh?" Clay's words didn't make any sense to her. I'm losing it, Pam thought. I'm totally losing it.

"My gun wasn't loaded," Clay repeated. "I just carried it for show."

"You didn't shoot him?"

"No way," Clay said, sighing loudly. "No way."

"That means—" Pam started, closing her eyes, trying to think.

"That means someone else killed the guard," Clay finished her sentence for her. "And someone else took the money."

"Clay, we've got to go to the police. We're not murderers. We didn't take anything. We've *got* to tell them the truth," Pam pleaded.

Clay didn't reply for a long moment. Then he said, "Pam—no one would believe us."

Chapter 18

ANOTHER PRESENT FOR REVA

"*P*lease! Please!" Michael begged. He lunged across Reva's bedroom, threw his skinny arms around her waist, and hugged her. "Please? You're the best sister! The best!"

Reva struggled out of his grasp. "Michael—give me a break!" she cried impatiently. "I'm trying to get dressed. You're going to make me late for work."

It was Monday morning, and Reva had promised her father that she'd be ready on time so that they could drive to the store together.

"But you promised!" Michael whined. "You promised!"

"I know I promised," Reva told him, studying her face in the mirror as she brushed her hair. "I'll take you to see Santa. Just not today."

"Why not?" he insisted, pouting comically, his hands on his hips like a crotchety old man.

"Because today isn't a good day," Reva said brusquely, adjusting her sweater, then stepping past him and striding out to the hallway.

"I've made my list," her brother called, chasing after her. He caught up with her at the head of the stairs, pushed his way past, and slid down the wooden banister. "Dad helped me. I said what I wanted, and he wrote it down."

"How many presents are on your list?" Reva asked, thinking about which coat to wear.

"Thirty, I think," he said. "That's why I've got to see Santa right away. Before he runs out of stuff."

Reva was only half listening. She was already wondering how she'd ever get through another long week behind the perfume counter. "Maybe tomorrow," she told her brother, patting him on the head. His curly red hair felt even softer and silkier than hers.

"You're a butt head," he said angrily and scrambled off to find Yvonne.

"Ready to go?" Mr. Dalby appeared in the hallway, already in his overcoat. His eyes were bloodshot and tired. His expression was troubled.

He's been obsessing about the break-in all weekend, Reva thought, allowing him to help her into her coat. I wish there was some way I could cheer him up.

They stepped out into a gray day, heavy, charcoal-colored clouds hovering low. "It's cold enough to snow," her father said, sniffing the air. "Smells like snow."

"We haven't had a white Christmas since I was little," Reva said, climbing into the passenger seat of the BMW.

"Sure you won't need your car today?" he asked, glancing at the silver Volvo in the garage.

"No. Maybe I'll wait around and come home with you," Reva said, settling into the seat. The heater came up right away, the air warm and soothing. Reva snuggled deeper into her coat, watching the familiar houses roll by in the gray morning light.

"I might be there awhile," Mr. Dalby said thoughtfully. "I mean, what with the robbery and all. I imagine there will be more police around today, more questions to answer. I talked to the insurance company for an hour on Saturday and two hours yesterday." He shook his head unhappily. "Can you imagine? On a Sunday? They were all upset because our surveillance wasn't working. I know my premiums are going up now."

They slowed for a four-way stop. Small, wet snowflakes began to fall onto the windshield, sticking for just a second before turning to water.

"What's their problem?" Reva asked, gazing at the windshield.

"There are just so many unanswered questions," Mr. Dalby said, driving with one gloved hand, scratching his smooth jaw with the other. "For instance, how did the robbers get into the store?"

"They broke in—right?" Reva asked.

They drove past her school, dark and empty. In

front someone had decorated one of the trees with a roll of toilet paper.

Kids are so immature, Reva thought.

"No, they didn't break in," her father said, his expression troubled. "There were no doors broken, no windows smashed. No sign of a break-in. And that's not the only question."

He slowed to a stop at Division Street and clicked on the windshield wipers. The snowflakes hitting the windshield were larger now, sticking longer.

"How did they know we had a safe on the first floor?" he asked, talking as much to himself as to Reva. "That safe is hidden. Very few people know about it. The main safe is on the sixth floor, in my office."

"So what do you think?" Reva asked. She hated to see her father so troubled, so upset.

"Well, I have to think it could have been an inside job," Mr. Dalby said, turning down the heat a little. "One of my employees. But that doesn't make sense, either. If it was an employee, they wouldn't have killed the guard, would they? Ed Javors was a friendly, well-liked guy. If the robber was an employee, he'd most likely know Ed. So I don't think he'd kill him."

"Strange," Reva said. They were nearly to the store.

"Javors was shot in the back," Mr. Dalby revealed, lowering his voice nearly to a whisper. "That doesn't make sense, either."

"How do you mean?" Reva asked.

"Let's say Javors entered the electronics department and discovered the burglary taking place. Why would he turn his back on the burglars?"

Maybe he was running away from them, Reva thought. But she didn't say it out loud. She didn't want to think about the robbery or the murdered guard. She had her own problems.

As if reading her thoughts, Mr. Dalby asked, "What was all over your sweater Friday? I've been so preoccupied with the robbery, I never talked with you about it. What a scare! I thought it was blood!"

It *was* blood, Reva thought. But she was determined not to upset her father any more than he already was.

"It was just a stupid practical joke someone played on me," she said.

Should she tell him she was pretty sure it was Hank? Should she ask him to get rid of Hank?

No. Reva wasn't the most thoughtful person in the world, but even she knew that this wasn't the time.

"Who?" he asked. "Who would do such a dumb thing during working hours?"

Reva shrugged. "Beats me."

"Well, I wish the person would stop," he said sternly. "I have enough trouble in the store without stupid jokes." He pulled into his private parking space, shifted into Park, and cut the engine. "Worst Christmas season I ever had," he muttered.

He was still muttering as Reva followed him up to his office. She gave him a quick kiss on the forehead, asked to deposit her coat in his closet, then headed back to the elevator to take her down to the main floor.

Hank was at his post in front of the bank of security monitors. He raised his head expectantly as she approached. But she cut him dead, sharply turning her face toward the opposite wall as she passed.

The morning dragged on forever. There were few customers even though it was so close to Christmas.

Ms. Smith wanted to discuss the horrible crime. "That poor guard. I knew him," she said, wringing her bony hands.

Reva tsk-tsked, but didn't add anything to the discussion.

At lunchtime she was surprised to see Mitch in front of her counter, wearing standard stockroom attire of faded jeans and a plain gray sweatshirt. "Reva—can I see you?" he asked, an urgent look on his face.

Reva smiled at him. "You're seeing me."

He didn't smile back. "No, I mean can I *talk* to you. In private." His eyes searched the long counter.

"Well, my supervisor just went to lunch," Reva said, studying his face, trying to figure out what he wanted to talk to her about so urgently. "I'm not supposed to leave till she gets back."

"It'll only take a few minutes," Mitch said, his dark eyes pleading with her.

"Well, okay. Wait a sec." Reva asked the salesgirl at the counter across from hers, a redhead named Mindy, to watch her booth. The young woman was reluctant, but Reva took Mitch's arm and hurried off without giving her a choice.

Mitch led her back to the electronics department. One aisle, the middle one, had been roped off by the police. Several police officers were in the department now, along with two photographers who seemed to be taking flash pictures of every display and counter.

The stockroom behind the electronics department was empty. Reva shivered as she followed Mitch to a low bench in the corner. It was at least twenty degrees colder in there than in the rest of the store.

"We keep the doors to the outside open," Mitch explained. "It makes it easier to work if you're a little cold."

"Fascinating," Reva said sarcastically. She sat down on a low bench. Mitch dropped down beside her and immediately reached for her, pressing his face up close to kiss her.

She let him kiss her for only a few seconds, then pulled her head away. "Aren't you afraid Lissa might walk in and catch us again?" she asked coyly.

He shook his head, a grin spreading across his face, the dimples appearing in his cheeks. "No. That's what I wanted to talk to you about, Reva."

"Well?"

"Well. Lissa broke up with me."

He stared at her, expecting a big reaction. But Reva decided not to give him the satisfaction. "Why'd she do that?" she asked, playing innocent.

"Because of you," he blurted out. "I mean, because of *me* and you."

That was easy, Reva thought, enjoying her triumph over Lissa secretly.

If only Mitch weren't such a wimp, she thought, I'd enjoy this even more. But the sight of him running after Lissa the other day, ready to beg Lissa to forgive him, had made Reva decide that Mitch wasn't worthy of her attention.

"That's too bad," she told Mitch, pouring on the sympathy in her voice.

"Huh?" His face filled with surprise at her reaction. "Well, Lissa was really mad. But I guess it's for the best," he said, recovering quickly. He put a hand on her shoulder. "I mean, after last week, I thought—well . . ."

She stared at him as if she had no idea what he was talking about.

"Well, since I'm not going with Lissa anymore," he continued uncertainly, "I thought maybe you and I could—uh—well, maybe go to a movie or something Saturday night."

Reva removed his hand from her shoulder and stood up. "No, I don't think so, Mitch," she said coldly.

"You have another date?"

"No," she said, her face hard and expressionless, not revealing how much she was enjoying herself. "I just don't think so."

She started to walk back to the selling floor, but he caught up with her and grabbed her arm. "You don't want to go out with me?"

"That's the general idea," she said flatly.

She stared hard at him until he let go of her arm and took a step back, his face red, his dark eyes wide with anger. "I don't get it," he said.

"That's right," she replied and smiled for the first time.

"You can't do this to people, Reva!" he screamed, starting to lose his temper.

"Looks like I just did," she told him smugly.

"You can't come on to somebody and—and—" Out of frustration at not being able to say what he wanted, he picked up the wooden bench they'd been sitting on and heaved it against the wall.

"Very impressive," Reva cracked. Ignoring his angry curses, she ambled slowly and deliberately from the stockroom without a glance back.

What a baby, she thought scornfully. What on earth did I ever see in him?

When she got back to the perfume counter, Mindy was on the phone. "It's for you," she told Reva after pushing the Hold button. "Your cousin Pam?"

Reva waved her hand, refusing to take the receiver. "Tell her I'm not in today," she said. "Tell her you haven't seen me."

Mindy hesitated for a moment, gave Reva a curious look, then spoke into the phone, giving Pam the message.

I don't feel like having a boring lunch with Pam today, Reva thought, glancing at the big clock on the far wall next to the Christmas tree. Pam is such a downer. She'll just want to complain about her life. She's always making me feel guilty for having more than she does.

Well, I'm just not in the mood to feel guilty today

Not about Mitch and Lissa. And not about Pam.

Mindy was off the phone now and hurrying across the aisle to her counter. "That package—it came for you," she called back to Reva, pointing.

Reva turned to see an enormous brown carton behind her in the cash register alcove. The carton was nearly as tall as she was. It wasn't gift wrapped, but it did have a wide red ribbon tied around it with a large bow on top.

Oh, no, Reva thought dispiritedly. Another stupid practical joke.

Who was doing this to her? What kind of dumb, obnoxious gag was it this time?

Shaking her head, she found a pair of scissors in the supply drawer beneath the register, cut open the carton, pulled back the lid, and peered inside.

It took her a second to realize that she was staring at a stiff, folded-up human corpse.

Then, still gripping the carton lid tightly with both hands, she started to scream.

Chapter 19

I SAW
WHAT YOU DID

Reva was still screaming when Ms. Smith appeared. She and Mindy pulled Reva away from the carton and peered inside.

"It's a mannequin!" Mindy shouted.

Reva didn't seem to hear.

"It's a mannequin. Only a mannequin," Ms. Smith repeated, taking Reva firmly by the shoulders.

"It sure *looks* real," Mindy said, shaking her head.

Reva, trembling all over, watched in silence as Mindy tilted the carton onto its side and pulled the lifelike mannequin out.

"Who sent this?" Ms. Smith snapped angrily, staring at Reva as if accusing her.

Reva was still too overcome to speak.

The mannequin stared up at Reva with wide, pale blue eyes, a wry smile painted on its face.

It looks as if it's laughing at me, Reva thought.

Everyone is laughing at me. I've made a complete fool of myself.

But it looked so real, so . . . dead.

"Look—there's a gift card!" Mindy exclaimed. She pulled a small white card off the mannequin's wrist.

Ms. Smith grabbed it out of Mindy's hand and tore open the envelope. She read it silently to herself, then held it up to Reva.

In scrawled block letters were the words: HAPPY HOLI-DAYS FROM A FRIEND.

What's going on here? Reva wondered, staring at the card. This isn't funny. This isn't funny at all.

When she raised her head, she noticed a blur of faces. The perfume counter was surrounded by a huge crowd of people, their expressions troubled, curious. All of them were staring at her.

"Who sent this?" Ms. Smith asked, her voice shrill and accusing. "Is this some kind of a joke?"

"What an awful joke," Mindy said with disgust.

The mannequin continued to stare up at Reva, the wry smile frozen on its pretty painted face.

The store suddenly got much noisier, the voices around her rising in a wave, as if the volume had been turned up. The circle of onlookers seemed to close in. The ceiling came crashing down. The floor rose up to meet it.

"No—please!"

Reva had to get away, away from the crowd, from

their eyes, their chattering voices. Away from the cold, staring body.

Straight-arming Mindy, she pushed out of the alcove and kept running.

"Reva! Reva!" She could hear Ms. Smith's shrill, alarmed voice behind her.

But she didn't stop, didn't turn around.

She kept running, running blindly through a blur of startled faces, not sure where she was running, just running away.

HAPPY HOLIDAYS FROM A FRIEND.

The words on the card followed her down the aisle.

Someone is trying to frighten me, she realized.

Someone is trying to terrify me.

Who could it be? she wondered. And why? Why are they doing this?

And just how far will they go?

Mr. Wakely, the collar of his worn leather jacket pulled up around his neck, padded through the living room and stopped at the front door. "You kids need anything, help yourselves," he said.

"Thanks, Mr. Wakely," Pam said uneasily. She was sitting on the edge of the worn couch, Clay beside her. Mickey was standing at the window, staring out at the snow-covered trees.

"Where you going, Dad?" Mickey asked. "The roads are pretty slick."

"Just down to the corner for a few beers," Mr. Wakely replied, pulling open the door. "I think I can make it. I'm not entirely feeble, you know," he added sharply.

He slammed the door behind him. Through the window, Mickey watched him make his way down the drive on foot, heading no doubt to Pat's, a dreary little bar just half a block away.

"Has he improved any?" Pam asked Mickey. "His spirits, I mean?"

Mickey shook his head. "He goes out for his beers now instead of downing them at the kitchen table. Call that an improvement?"

He continued to stand at the window for a while longer, then joined his friends across the room. He slouched low into a folding chair and sighed. "I keep expecting a knock on the door," he said quietly.

"You mean the police?" Pam asked, automatically checking the door.

"Yeah," Mickey replied. "It's been three days. I can't figure out why we haven't been caught yet."

"Maybe we're not going to get caught," Clay said, breaking his silence. He'd been staring at his sneakers since he'd arrived about an hour before. "Maybe we got away with it." He narrowed his gray eyes and stared at Mickey as if challenging him.

Mickey glanced at Pam and didn't say anything.

"We got away with murder," Pam muttered, thinking out loud.

"We didn't murder anybody!" Clay insisted loudly, jumping to his feet and pacing. "I *told* you—my gun wasn't loaded."

"Sit down, Clay," Pam said, slapping the couch cushion. "I only meant—"

"Somebody else killed the guard," Clay said heatedly, jamming his fists into his jeans pockets. He wouldn't say anything more.

"And somebody got twenty-five thousand dollars," Mickey added glumly.

"Yeah. And we left with what we came in with—nothing!" Clay shouted, working himself up into a rage.

"Did you talk to Maywood?" Pam asked calmly, her hands clasped nervously in her lap. "Did you find out what happened to him Friday night?"

Clay shook his head as he paced to the window, taking Mickey's old spot and staring out at the thin layer of new snow. Less than an inch had fallen during the day. "I tried calling him at Dalby's. They said he called in sick. When I tried his apartment, there was no answer."

"If he was sick, wouldn't he have called you?" Pam asked, playing nervously with the frayed fabric on the couch arm. "I just don't understand why he let us go through with the robbery if he knew he wasn't going to be there. I mean, if he knew it was going to be a different guard, why wouldn't he—"

"How should I know?" Clay interrupted wildly. "Give me a break, will you?"

"Pam wasn't accusing you or anything!" Mickey cried, coming to Pam's defense.

"You both think it's my fault the thing got messed

153

up," Clay said, his eyes darting back and forth between them. "Well, there was nothing I could do." He moved to the center of the room, breathing hard, his chest heaving.

"We don't blame you," Mickey said, trying to calm Clay. Mickey was obviously frightened—he knew what Clay could be like if he lost control.

"Look, we're all in this together—right?" Pam quickly added. "Come on, Clay. Sit down."

He crossed his arms over his chest, refusing to budge.

"Did you call your cousin?" Mickey asked Pam. "Does her father suspect anything? Does he know anything?"

"I tried to reach her around lunchtime. But the girl at the perfume counter said she wasn't there," Pam said, making an annoyed face. "I think I heard her in the background before I was put on Hold. She just didn't want to talk to me."

"Because she knows that you—that we—" Mickey couldn't finish his question.

"Nobody knows anything," Clay insisted loudly, as if trying to convince himself. "If anybody thought it was us there Friday night, we wouldn't be sitting here talking about it. We'd be in a hot little room somewhere, being grilled by the cops."

"Clay's right," Mickey said, brightening. "It's obvious that no one saw us. No one has any idea we were there."

The phone beside the couch rang.

Pam, startled, picked it up. "Hello?"

The voice on the other end was gruff, hoarse. "I saw what you did," he rasped.

"What?" Pam froze.

"I saw what you did," the voice croaked, low and menacing. "I want my share."

"No!" Pam shrieked and dropped the phone.

Chapter 20

I'LL KILL HIM

"Where were you last night?" Foxy asked.

Pam hesitated for a moment. "I told you. I went over to Mickey's," she said uneasily, avoiding his eyes. "I offered to help him and Clay. They've got a big math project due at the end of vacation."

"Oh. I didn't remember." Foxy stared at her thoughtfully, pulling at the neck of his blue sweater. "Are you okay, Pam?"

"Yeah. Fine," she lied, forcing a smile. She squeezed his arm tenderly, reassuring him.

He knows me too well, she thought. He can tell that something is troubling me. If only I could tell him. But I won't. No way. No way I want to get him involved.

It was Tuesday night. Pam's parents were out grocery shopping, and she and Foxy were sitting on the living-room couch. Some sitcom was on the TV across the room, but neither of them was paying any attention to it.

"How's work?" Pam asked, trying to change the subject, trying to get Foxy to stop studying her so intently.

He shrugged. "Not bad. It has its enjoyable moments," he said. "How come you've been hanging out with Clay and Mickey so much?"

She smiled at him, trying to cover up her uneasiness. "Foxy, you're not the jealous type, are you?" she asked, taking his big hand between hers.

"Maybe," he replied, returning her smile.

"It's just that you've been so busy," she told him, trying not to sound defensive.

He started to say something, but the phone rang.

She got up, crossed the room to turn down the sound on the TV, then picked up the phone from the low table near the hallway.

She recognized the gruff voice immediately.

"I want my share," he whispered in her ear.

He knows where I live! Pam thought. He knows who I am!

She glanced across the room at Foxy, who was watching her who must have seen the horror on her face.

"I want ten thousand dollars or I'm telling the police," the voice rasped.

"What do you mean?" Pam asked, her voice trembling. She turned toward the wall, hoping Foxy wouldn't hear.

"I saw you," the voice said. "I saw you kill the guard. I saw everything."

"No—we didn't!" Pam shrieked. "We didn't do it!"

Across the room Foxy jumped to his feet.

The caller ignored Pam's outburst. "I want ten thousand dollars to keep quiet," he rasped. "I'll be coming for it soon."

"But we don't *have* any money!" Pam cried.

She was talking to a dead phone line. He had already clicked off.

"Pam—"

She was startled to discover that Foxy was standing right behind her.

"Pam—what is it? Who *was* that?"

"Oh, Foxy!" she cried and fell into his arms.

He hugged her close. "What? What? Tell me," he insisted.

"I'm so scared," she confessed, her head against his chest. "So scared."

"Who was that?" he repeated. "What's happening, Pam?"

She had to tell him. She was too frightened to hold it in any longer.

He led her back to the couch, and they sat down. He held her hands tightly. "Foxy, you're not going to like this," she began and then told him the whole story.

She started with the night at Mickey's when Clay revealed his plan for robbing Dalby's. With a trembling voice she told him about the robbery, how it went wrong, how the guard was shot, how they fled and just narrowly escaped before the police arrived.

Even though they were alone in the house, she whispered, leaning in close to him. All the time she talked she studied his face for the disapproval she knew would be there.

But Foxy's face revealed only concern, concern mixed with disbelief. He listened to the whole story in silence. Then, when she finished telling him about the raspy voice demanding ten thousand dollars, he let go of her, his expression changed, his dark eyebrows lowered over his dark eyes.

"Pam," he said, "I-I'm so—sorry."

She had managed to hold herself together till then. But now her shoulders heaved, and she began to sob.

Foxy reached out to comfort her, but she pushed him away. She wanted to cry. She wanted to sob and scream and kick. She'd been holding it in too long, much too long.

But to Pam's surprise, the feeling passed quickly. She dried her cheeks with her hands. She smiled guiltily at Foxy and apologized.

"I didn't want you to know any of this," she admitted. "I wasn't going to tell you."

"I'm not surprised about Clay," Foxy said thoughtfully. "But you and Mickey—"

"I just got so tired of being poor!" Pam cried. "And so—so jealous of Reva, I guess. I don't know, Foxy. I mean, I have no excuse. I was stupid. I went along with it."

She stood up suddenly, gripped by one thought. "What am I going to do now? This creep who just called—he knows where I live. He—he's very frightening, Foxy."

"You have to go to the police. Tell them everything. Just what you told me," Foxy said.

"No, I can't!" she shouted. "Don't you see? The police won't believe us! I'm amazed that *you* do!"

"But, Pam—"

"No!" She cut him off firmly. "We can't tell the police that we were there but didn't kill the guard or take the money. They wouldn't believe us in a million years. Besides, Clay would never agree to go to the police."

Foxy got up off the couch and grabbed Pam's hand. "Let's go see Clay," he said.

A few minutes later they were in her mother's car, driving toward Mickey's house, where Clay and Mickey were hanging out as usual. Earlier in the day the snow had started to melt. Then the temperature dropped again and the roads froze over.

Foxy gripped the passenger door handle tightly as the car slipped across the ice. "Can't you drive a little slower?" he asked nervously.

"I'm only going fifteen," Pam told him, "and I'm still sliding all over. It's really treacherous. Maybe we should turn around and go back."

"No," he insisted. "We're almost there. We've got to talk to Clay and Mickey and figure out what you're going to do about this . . . blackmailer."

"You're being very understanding about this whole thing," Pam said, pulling out of a skid.

"I'm a saint—remember?" Foxy cracked, holding on to the door handle for dear life.

They slid most of the way to Mickey's house where Pam parked by the curb. To walk up to the front door, they had to lean into the frigid north wind.

Mickey was surprised when he saw Foxy. "Hi, how's it going?" he asked Foxy, staring at Pam.

"He knows," Pam told Mickey. "I told him all about it."

"Let us in. It's freezing out here!" Foxy cried.

"It isn't much warmer in here," Mickey said, shaking his head. "I don't think Dad paid the heating bill."

They stepped into the small living room. "Yo, join the party," Clay said glumly.

"Clay, I got another phone call," Pam said anxiously, the words spilling out of her. "The same guy with the croaky voice. He says he wants ten thousand dollars. He says he saw us in the store. He says he's coming for his ten thousand real soon."

Clay didn't react at first, just stared intently at the window. Then he looked up at Pam and in a low, calm voice said, "Whoever he is, I'll *kill* him."

The quiet way Clay said that frightened Pam as much as anything that had happened. It was something people said all the time. "I'll kill him. I swear, I'll kill him." It was something said in anger. An empty expression. People never really meant it.

161

With Clay it was different. Clay didn't say things he didn't mean. It was one of the scary things about him.

"Clay—you're kidding, right?" Pam said, more of a plea than a question. "Please—promise me you're kidding."

Chapter 21

EVERYONE HATES YOU, REVA

Thursday morning, even though she was an hour late, Reva rode up to the sixth floor, hung her coat in her father's closet, then strode quickly to the bank of security monitors to talk to Hank.

She tapped him on the shoulder hard, and he whirled away from the screens. "Reva. Hi." He eyed her suspiciously. The last time she had passed, she cut him dead.

"Hank, it's time to stop the stupid games," she said, her voice low and hard. She had practiced her speech all the way to the store. She knew exactly what she wanted to say.

"Reva, I can't talk right now," he told her, glancing back at the screens. "The store is open. I'm supposed to monitor these screens."

She grabbed his arm and tugged, pulling him off the high stool. "Hey, let go—" he protested unconvincingly. "What's your problem, anyway, Reva?"

"This will only take a few seconds," she said.

"But my job—"

"You won't lose your job. I promise," she said, her face still cold and expressionless. She pulled him into her father's office, which was empty, and closed the door.

"Reva. Listen—" He stared into her eyes, trying to figure out what she wanted.

"No more games," Reva repeated, brushing back her hair. "Stop playing innocent, Hank. I'm not buying it."

"Innocent?" He shifted his weight uncomfortably, shoving his hands into the pockets of his blue uniform trousers.

"Look, I guess I was pretty cruel to you," she continued with her speech. "I mean, I said some things I shouldn't have. And that night with the guard dog. Well—I apologize."

He continued to study her face, his expression unchanging.

"I hope you'll accept my apology," Reva went on, returning his stare, "because I'm asking you for a truce now. I want you to stop trying to frighten me."

"Huh?" His mouth dropped open in exaggerated surprise.

"You heard me," she said sharply. "I want you to stop all the stupid jokes. They're not funny, and they're getting out of control."

Hank shook his head. He removed his hands from his pockets and raked one back through his spiky, blond hair. "Have you totally lost it, or what?"

"Hank!" She didn't want to lose her temper. But she couldn't help it. "I know you're the one who sent me the dummy in the box. And the bottle of blood."

"Huh?"

"You're not a good liar, Hank," Reva said, glaring angrily at him. "You put a needle in my lipstick. You've been trying to frighten me, trying to terrorize me to pay me back for the way I broke up with you. But—"

"No way," he said softly. He took a step toward the closed office door. "No way."

"You're denying it?" Her eyes burned into his.

"No way," he repeated.

"Hank, I know you hate me," Reva blurted out. She surprised herself. That wasn't in her prepared speech.

It appeared to surprise Hank too. His expression changed, softened. His dark eyes narrowed. "Hey, I don't hate you," he said. "I feel sorry for you."

His words stung like a slap in the face. She uttered a low cry. *"You* feel sorry for *me?"* She felt like laughing and crying at the same time. "I don't understand," she managed to say, confused by her strong feelings.

"Anyone could have sent you those things," Hank explained. "You don't have a friend in the world, Reva. Everyone hates you. Everyone. I can think of *ten* people who hate you enough to put a needle in your lipstick."

"You're crazy!" she screamed. "You're really sick!"

165

"I'm not saying it to be cruel," he replied heatedly, his normally pale face flushed, his dark eyes excited. "I'm explaining why I feel sorry for you."

"But it's not true—" Reva started.

"Tell me one good friend you've got," Hank demanded, moving toward her, looming over her, powerful in his blue uniform. "Come on. Name one."

"Well—"

Why couldn't she think of anyone?

How stupid, she thought. Of course I have friends. I have lots of friends.

Name one, Reva, she challenged herself. Name one.

"I feel sorry for you," Hank repeated, not backing off, not letting her off the hook. "You don't have a friend in the world."

Reva let her head drop.

She raised it and stared at Hank. He was right.

She felt deflated, as if someone had popped her with a pin and everything holding her together had been blown apart.

"You're right, Hank," she said, her voice a whisper.

He stared back at her expectantly, waiting for her to continue.

"Ever since Mom died, I—I haven't had time for friends. I had to be hard," she said, talking more to herself than to Hank. "I had to keep to myself. Keep my feelings to myself. I knew if I let my feelings go for one second, I'd lose control and—and—"

Her voice caught in her throat.

They stared at each other, standing close together now.

Hank's expression softened, his dark eyes searching her face.

"I—I didn't even cry at Mom's funeral," Reva said. "Even then, I knew I had to hold myself in, had to harden myself. Otherwise—"

Before Reva knew it, she was in Hank's arms. He felt so warm, so strong, so protective.

But even now, pressing her face against his, feeling his arms wrap tighter around her, she couldn't cry, didn't want to cry.

And even now, allowing herself to be comforted, allowing Hank to hold her, allowing herself to let go just a bit, to loosen the reins that had held her in so tightly, even now Reva felt the fear.

Even now she wondered if Hank wasn't the one trying to frighten her. Even now she wondered: What's next?

Pam slammed down the phone.

No answer at Reva's house. And the line was still busy at Foxy's.

Who could he be talking to all this time?

She glanced at her watch. It was eight thirty-five. Thursday night.

She still wanted to talk to Reva, to find out what was being said in the store, if there were any theories as to who the culprits were who robbed the store and killed the guard.

But Reva obviously wasn't home. And Foxy—what was Foxy doing on the phone all this time? Talking to some secret girlfriend?

The thought tickled her. She couldn't imagine Foxy sneaking around with another girl.

But, she realized, anything was possible. She couldn't imagine herself burglarizing a department store. And yet she had.

I'm going to go see what Foxy is doing, she decided.

She pushed open the storm door and peered out across her small square of a front yard. It was warm out, almost springlike. The ice and snow had all melted. The air smelled fresh and piney.

Pam decided to walk to Foxy's. It was only five blocks. She hadn't had any exercise all day, having hung around the house, unable to do anything or concentrate on anything but how sorry she felt for herself.

Foxy's being so understanding about this, she thought, crossing the street and walking with quick strides along the sidewalk past familiar, silent houses. He seemed to realize right away that I didn't need him to scold me or disapprove of me or tell me what an idiot I was.

He's been so supportive, like a real friend.

And he's so cute and cuddly.

A lot of girls wouldn't appreciate Foxy, she thought. But I knew right away that he was special.

Two blocks later she was smiling to herself, thinking about Foxy, when the hand grabbed her from behind.

Before she could scream, the gloved hand slid down over her mouth, holding her too tight to scream.

She tried to pull away, but overwhelmed by panic, her muscles locked, all of her strength seemed to die.

She felt hot breath against her cheek.

Another arm was now locked tightly around her waist.

She was being dragged, dragged off the sidewalk into a dark yard, behind a tall hedge where no one could see her. No one could help.

Chapter 22

WHAT ARE YOU GOING TO DO TO ME?

I can't breathe, Pam thought.

I'm too terrified to breathe.

Who is it? What is he going to do?

The tall hedge seemed to surround her, bend in on her, suffocate her.

Don't panic. Don't panic. Don't panic.

Got to think.

Got to find a way to get free.

Her eyes darted to the house above the sloping lawn. Please—somebody be there. Somebody—help me.

But the house was dark. The curtains were pulled.

The gloved hand loosened a little over her mouth.

"Don't scream. Don't try to turn around." The raspy voice was right in her ear.

Again she felt his breath, hot and wet against her cheek.

He shoved her then, into the prickly hemlock hedge, still holding on to her.

"I'm warning you. Don't turn around. Don't yell for help."

I'm too scared to yell, Pam thought. I'm too scared to make a sound.

She was breathing hard now, breathing noisily through her nose.

The gloved hand slipped away from her mouth, and she gasped, sucking in big mouthfuls of air.

"Don't turn around and you won't get hurt," the voice whispered, just behind her.

"What are you going to do to me?" Pam managed to cry.

There was a long silence.

Somewhere down the block a car door slammed. A dog barked.

"What are you going to do to me?" Pam repeated, her voice so filled with terror she didn't recognize it.

On the other side of the thick hedge a car rolled slowly past.

Can't you see me? Pam thought, watching the headlights through the shrub. Please, driver—please see me.

But the car moved silently by. The lights disappeared.

The grip tightened around her waist. "I saw what you did," the voice whispered. "I was there Friday night."

"But I don't have any money," Pam whispered back. "We—"

"Don't turn around!" he rasped. "I'm warning you."

They were both breathing hard now.

Pam became cold all over, numb, frozen with fear. "Please—" she said.

"This is just a warning," he said, not loosening his grip. "I can get to you. Easy. I can hurt you. I can hurt you *right now."*

"What do you want me to do?" Pam whispered, staring at the dark ground.

"I want ten thousand dollars. That's all. And I want it tomorrow night."

"But I'm trying to tell you," Pam whispered, choking out the words, "we don't have the money. We didn't take any money. *Ow!"*

She screamed as both his hands dug into her waist, and he pushed her face into the hedge.

"Don't lie to me! I was there! I saw you!"

"I'm not lying!" Pam insisted.

"I want ten thousand dollars tomorrow night, or I'm going to the police. Do you hear me?"

Instead of replying, Pam took a deep breath. Then, with a burst of strength, she ducked low and twisted out of his grasp. With a cry she lurched away from the hedge and stumbled down the drive to the street.

And spun around.

And saw who it was.

Pam recognized him immediately.

"You!" she cried. "I don't believe it!"

His eyes flashed with fear for just a moment, then anger drove out all other expression.

As she gaped at him in shock, he caught up with her, grabbed her by the shoulders, and tossed her hard to the asphalt driveway.

He stood over her, then dropped down, pinning her to the drive.

"Too bad you turned around," he whispered.

Chapter 23

ANOTHER PRACTICAL JOKE

*E*verything went white.

Pam shut her eyes.

When she reopened them, the light was still there. As she stared into it, it seemed to divide in two.

It took her a few seconds to realize she was looking at car headlights, moving slowly toward her.

Where was her attacker?

He was already running away. She spotted him darting along the hedges, keeping low until he reached the corner. Then he turned and disappeared in the heavy darkness.

Pam got to her knees, and the earth seemed to tilt and spin.

Still on the ground, she raised a hand and waved to the car. It stopped. The door on the driver's side opened.

"Here—please!" she managed to cry.

Stand up, she told herself.

But the ground was too slanted. She wasn't sure she could get all the way up.

She heard footsteps, heavy, hurried footsteps. Then two hands had her by the shoulders.

"Pam?"

She raised her head, tried to focus. "Foxy!"

Confused and concerned, he held on to her. "Pam —what's going on? Who was that?"

She shook her head.

The ground was tilting back to normal. The hedges weren't spinning quite so rapidly.

"Foxy—I'm so glad to see you," she managed to say.

She allowed him to pull her to her feet. Then she leaned against him as he walked her to his car.

"Who was that? I saw someone running," he said, supporting her against his side.

"Foxy," she said, "you won't *believe* who is black-mailing us. You just won't believe it!"

The next morning Reva congratulated herself on arriving at the store on time. In fact, she was there ten minutes before the doors opened.

I hope I'm not turning over a new leaf, she thought. Promptness is such a boring virtue.

It was bound to be a busy day, she realized. The Friday before Christmas meant that last-minute shoppers would be thronging the store. On her way in she had seen a line of people, huddling against the morning cold, waiting for the doors to open.

Reva decided a busy day would suit her just fine. Maybe having to wait on a lot of customers would keep her mind occupied so she could stop thinking about her conversation with Hank.

She had thought of little else since the day before. At first she had thought Hank was being cruel. But the more she considered what he said, the more she realized that he had spoken out of concern for her.

And she decided that he might have been right.

She had always thought there was something stupid and thickheaded about Hank. But that was only because it was necessary for her to feel superior to other people. Hank, she knew now, was a lot more sensitive than she had given him credit for.

Could it really be Hank who was playing these disgusting, cruel jokes on her?

Reva couldn't think about that now.

She had been pacing around the first floor as she thought and had made her way to the electronics department when she heard shouting in the electronics stockroom.

Reva stopped.

She heard loud cursing and then grunts and groans, shoes scraping against concrete, boxes falling, the sounds of people scuffling.

She hurried to the doorway of the stockroom and peered in.

"Hey—" she cried in alarm. "What's going on? Stop it!"

The two boys wrestling in the middle of the floor ignored her and didn't even look up once from their fight.

"Mitch—what on earth!" Reva cried.

Mitch, red-faced, his thick, black hair wild about his face, was wrestling with Robb, who was in full Santa costume, except for the beard and red hat, which were on the floor.

"Stop it! Come *on*—stop it!" Reva pleaded.

The two boys continued to ignore her, cursing each other angrily as they rolled on the floor, throwing wild punches.

Reva stormed to the middle of the floor, leaned down, and tried to pull Robb off Mitch. But he wriggled out of her grasp and landed a hard punch on Mitch's jaw.

"What's going on here?"

All three of them turned around as Donald Rawson, the stockroom manager, burst into the room. Rawson reacted quickly and strode over to the struggling boys. He quickly pulled Robb away.

Mitch climbed slowly to his feet, rubbing his already swollen cheek. "Robb's crazy," he told Rawson. "He started it—for no reason."

Robb glared silently at Mitch, gulping air, his face nearly as red as his costume.

"I don't want to hear about it," Rawson said angrily. "Just get to work." He turned to Robb. "Pick up your stuff and get your costume together. The doors are opening in less than five minutes."

"But he—" Mitch started.

177

Rawson raised a hand to cut him off. "I *said* I don't want to hear about it. Settle it after work, okay? Go out to the parking lot and beat each other senseless. But at least wait until Robb is out of costume—okay? That's all we need is for kids to see the Dalby's Santa Claus in a fistfight with a stock clerk!"

The two boys looked as if they wanted to continue their fight, but Rawson stood between them, waiting with his arms crossed. Finally Robb bent down and picked up his costume pieces before lumbering out of the stockroom.

"I don't believe you guys," Rawson muttered to Mitch. Then he, too, hurried out.

Mitch avoided Reva's stare. He was still rubbing his swollen cheek.

"What was *that* all about?" Reva asked, shaking her head, bewildered.

Mitch shrugged. "What do *you* care?" he muttered. Then he headed over to the crates in the receiving area and started to unstack them.

Reva watched him for a few seconds before heading for the main floor.

Is everyone going crazy? she wondered.

"I couldn't find my list, but I still remember everything I want," Michael said excitedly.

Holding his hand tightly, Reva led her little brother through an aisle mobbed with late-afternoon shoppers. As they climbed the short flight of stairs, Santa Land came into view, a long line of kids against one wall, clinging to their parents, hopping up and down, chattering excitedly.

"Ooh—there he is!" Michael exclaimed, his eyes lighting up.

"We have to wait in line," Reva said, pointing to where they had to go.

"Is that beard real?" Michael asked, staring at Robb as he lifted a crying little girl off his lap.

"Why don't you ask him?" Reva replied, laughing.

"No. I'm just going to ask for presents," Michael said seriously.

They stepped to the end of the line. A tiny little girl, two at the most, was seated on Robb's lap, tugging hard on his beard.

"Do I have to sit on his lap?" Michael asked, and he seemed anxious all of a sudden about the experience he'd been looking forward to. "Couldn't I just stand up next to him?"

Robb would probably appreciate that, Reva thought. But she told Michael, "No. It's a law. You have to sit on his lap if you want to get the presents you ask him for."

Michael thought about this earnestly, biting his lower lip.

Reva laughed at how serious he appeared and ran her hand through his silky red hair. "You don't want to hurt Santa's feelings, do you? He likes boys and girls to sit on his lap," she said.

He likes it about as much as a toothache, she thought, chuckling.

The line inched forward. Kids were climbing all over their parents, impatient to get their Santa visit over with. Several mothers fussed with cameras, ignoring the squawking kids at their feet.

Finally Michael was next in line. "Do you think he knows my name?" he asked Reva, still grasping her hand.

"I think you should tell him your name," Reva suggested.

"What about my address? Does Santa know my address?"

Before Reva could answer, one of Santa's elves, a young woman in a truly ridiculous costume with bells on her cap and on her soft, pointy shoes, came to usher Michael up to Santa's throne.

He immediately let go of Reva's hand and half walking, half skipping followed the elf, an eager smile on his face.

I should have brought a camera too, Reva thought, moving out of the line to the waiting area on the other side of Santa Land. Daddy should see this.

She watched Michael as he made himself comfortable on Santa's lap, listing all of the things he "needed" for Christmas, counting them off endlessly on his fingers. He had indeed memorized his entire list.

When he was finally finished, he ran back to meet Reva, perplexed. "That Santa's a fake," he told her.

"Huh?" She took his hand. "What are you talking about?"

"It's not his real stomach. There's a pillow in there. I felt it."

"Well, he's just Santa's helper," Reva explained, guiding him toward the elevators. "The real Santa is up at the North Pole. But Santa's helpers get all of the information up to the real Santa in time."

This seemed to satisfy her brother. Feeling glad that she'd finally kept her promise to him, Reva dropped Michael off on the sixth floor at her father's office. Then, humming to herself, she returned to the perfume counter.

There, behind the counter, she found another enormous carton waiting for her. Like the one before, it, too, was tied in a broad red ribbon with a bow on the top.

Reva sighed. "When did this come?" she asked Ms. Smith.

"Please—I'm with a customer," her supervisor snapped. "Some of us here actually wait on customers."

Another stupid, mean trick, Reva thought, staring at the big carton.

Only this time I'm not going to scream and carry on.

I'd have to be pretty stupid to fall for the same thing twice in a row.

She snipped the ribbon with a pair of scissors, then cut off the tape that secured the lid.

Someone has a really juvenile sense of humor, she told herself.

Sick and juvenile.

I suppose another poor mannequin has been sacrificed in an attempt to scare me to death.

She pulled back the lid and stared inside.

And froze.

Her breath caught in her throat. She started to choke.

She spun her head away, but the sight didn't leave. It seemed to be burned into her eyes.

This was no mannequin.

No mannequin. No mannequin. No mannequin.

It was Mitch crumpled up in the bottom of the carton.

And the blood that had dripped down his back and made a small puddle on the carton floor was real.

Because there was a large kitchen knife shoved between Mitch's shoulder blades.

Chapter 24

WHO MURDERED MITCH?

*E*very time Reva closed her eyes, she saw Mitch.

Saw his knees pressed against the side of the carton, rising up over his bowed head.

Saw his shoulders sloped forward in the carton, arms hanging limply at his sides.

Saw the back of his neck, so pale. His shiny black hair, usually so carefully brushed, matted against his head.

Saw the dark stain on the back of his shirt. The puddle of coagulated blood on the carton bottom, soaking through his jeans.

Saw the knife handle, the tiny gleam of blade protruding from it, placed so perfectly, so symmetrically in the middle of his shoulder blades.

Every time Reva closed her eyes, she saw all of this.

And when her eyes were open, she couldn't see

clearly, couldn't think clearly, couldn't think of anything else.

When the police questioned her, two soft-spoken police officers, one not much older than Reva, she couldn't think, could barely speak.

Why would anyone murder Mitch?

Why would someone murder Mitch and gift wrap him for her?

Reva had no answers.

And there was Lissa, leaning her head on the glass of the perfume counter, sobbing and smearing the glass with her tears.

She couldn't help the police, either.

After the questions, after what seemed like hours of police milling and poking around, after the photographers, after the reporters, the paramedics, the hushed crowds of muttering onlookers, after the bent, lifeless body had been covered and carried away, and the carton had been dragged away, leaving a wide scum of blood in its wake, Reva still saw the body, still saw poor, slumped-over Mitch.

She remembered kissing him in the stockroom.

She remembered Lissa breaking in on them.

She remembered laughing at Mitch after Lissa broke up with him.

And she saw Lissa, her face red and puffy from crying so long, cast an accusing glance at Reva.

Accusing. Deserved.

I owe Mitch an apology, Reva thought. But it's too late. Too late to tell him I'm sorry.

And for the first time in years, Reva felt like crying.

Felt like it but still managed to hold the tears in.

"Go home," her father said gently, his warm hands on her trembling shoulders. "Shall I have someone drive you home?"

"No. It's okay. I'll be okay," she said, reaching up to squeeze his hand.

I'll never be okay, she thought.

At home that evening she kept seeing Mitch, kept apologizing to him in her mind.

That night she forced him away, forced herself to fall into a deep sleep. A sleep of troubling dreams, complicated and violent.

Just before two in the morning Reva sat straight up, wide awake. "I know who killed Mitch," she said aloud.

Chapter 25

HE'S JUST A WORM

"Clay—did you kill Mitch?"

Sprawled on Mickey's couch, Clay looked up at Pam, the smile fading from his face.

"Did you?" Pam demanded, standing over him, her hands on her hips. "Did you kill him?"

The wind rattled the loose pane in the living-room window. Mickey stepped out of the shadows of the darkened kitchen and turned on the floor lamp next to the couch. His face was drawn, Pam saw, his eyes tense, wary. He held a half-eaten Three Musketeers in his left hand, but wasn't chewing on it.

Clay still didn't reply. "Give me a break, Pam," he muttered, rolling his eyes.

"I'm not going to let you off the hook," Pam said. "I want to know, Clay. I *have* to know. After I told you that Mitch was the one who was blackmailing us, that

Mitch was the one who grabbed me and threatened me—did you go to the store and kill him?"

"Of *course* he didn't," Mickey interrupted, speaking with unusual fervor. But he sounded more hopeful than convinced. "Tell her, Clay," he urged. "Stop being so stubborn."

Clay snickered. "She's accusing me of murder, and you accuse me of being stubborn," he said wryly. "I really don't believe this."

"Well, Mitch is dead," Pam said heatedly, crossing her arms over her chest, refusing to retreat from her position, glaring down at Clay. "And he was murdered."

"So?" Clay asked, his gray eyes flashing angrily. "You think I did it?"

"Yeah," Mickey agreed. "What makes you think it was Clay who did it?"

"Because he *said* he'd do it," she told Mickey impatiently. "Clay said when he found out who was threatening us, he'd kill him." She turned back to Clay, who now had a smile on his face.

"What if I did kill him?" he asked.

"Did you?" Pam insisted.

He shrugged, his smile insolent, defiant.

Pam glanced over at Mickey, who was still standing at the lamp. In the yellow light he looked frightened. "Clay—?" He let the candy bar drop from his hand. It landed noiselessly on the worn carpet. Staring hard at Clay, he didn't bother to pick it up.

Clay ignored him, continuing to smirk at Pam.

187

"You didn't kill him—*did* you?" Mickey asked, his voice frightened and small. "Come on, man. Just say you didn't, okay?"

"Okay. I didn't," Clay said, still smirking.

"I don't believe you," Pam said. She glanced over at Mickey. It was obvious that Mickey had changed his mind about Clay. He didn't believe Clay, either.

"Hey, come on, guys," Clay said, pushing himself up on his feet from the low couch. He took a step forward, rolling down the sleeve of his black Motley Crue T-shirt, forcing Pam to back away. "Get out of my face, okay? I'm telling you the truth. I didn't croak Mitch—all right?"

He walked to the window and stared out into the tiny front yard. "I wanted to," he said, his back to them. "When I found out he was in the store that night watching us the whole time, I wanted to kill him. But then I thought about it, you know. And I decided he wasn't worth it. He was just a worm. Why should I mess up my life on account of a worm?"

Mickey picked up his candy bar and tossed it onto the low table by the wall. He and Pam exchanged glances. They were each trying to decide whether to believe Clay or not.

"I hope you're telling the truth, man," Mickey said walking up close to Clay. "Because if you're lying, we—"

Without warning, Clay spun around and grabbed the front of Mickey's gray sweatshirt. He jerked it violently, nearly pulling Mickey off his feet. "I'm not a liar!" he screamed, his features hard and menacing.

At that moment Mr. Wakely stepped into the room from the dark kitchen. "Hey—" He seemed surprised by the violent confrontation across the room.

Clay immediately let go of Mickey's sweatshirt, and Mickey stumbled backward quickly regaining his balance.

Mr. Wakely stood blinking in the light. Pam could see that his eyes were red rimmed and bloodshot. He was stooped and unsteady on his legs. It was obvious he'd been drinking.

He's aged ten years in just the past week, Pam thought.

"Get out of here if you're going to fight!" he screamed, shaking his fist at Mickey. "Get out! Get out!"

He lunged toward Mickey and nearly fell over his own feet.

He's totally out of control, Pam thought. There's no reason for him to be so angry at Mickey.

"We were just going out, Dad," Mickey said, backing off. "Come on, guys."

They grabbed their coats and a few seconds later were standing out front, shivering in the swirling winter wind.

"Sorry about Dad," Mickey apologized, obviously embarrassed. "I don't know what his problem is." He kicked at a rock at the curb, shooting it across the street.

"I'm outta here," Clay said glumly. "Unless you

want to call the cops on me and turn me in for killing Mitch." He glared at Pam and Mickey, challenging them.

"You didn't do it," Mickey said softly. "I know you didn't do it, man."

That odd smile returned to Clay's face, the smile Pam couldn't interpret, the one that sent a cold chill down her spine.

Chapter 26

A CONFESSION

Saturday morning Reva woke up early and quickly slipped into a pair of gray wool slacks and a cream-colored cashmere pullover. She hurried downstairs, brushing her hair as she walked, eager that her father didn't leave without her.

In the breakfast room her dad raised his eyes from his cup of coffee, surprised. "You're up early for a Saturday," he said, studying her. "If you're not careful, you'll get to work on time this morning."

Reva didn't smile at his little joke. "I didn't want to miss you," she said seriously. "I have an idea—about the murder."

The smile quickly faded from his face. He put down his coffee mug. "What's your idea?"

"I'll have to show you. When we get to the store," Reva said. "I'm not sure, but I may have a clue. It came to me in the middle of the night."

Reva had done a lot of thinking during the night, about the robbery, about Mitch, about Hank—and about herself. She wasn't happy about herself, she realized, about how hard, how cold she had become. But Mitch's murder and the feelings it had stirred in her had hinted that it wasn't too late—there was still some of the old Reva, hiding behind the hard shell she had built around herself.

She spooned down a bowl of cornflakes, grabbed her coat, and hurried out to the garage, where her father was already warming up the car. A red morning sun was climbing the sky. The air was still and cold. The lawn sparkled under a layer of frozen dew.

They drove to work in silence, listening to the all-news station on the radio. "What's your theory?" Mr. Dalby asked after he had parked the car in his reserved space and they were walking across the lot to the back entrance of the store.

"I have to show you," Reva said. "I don't mean to be mysterious, Daddy. I just have to make sure myself first."

They went up to the sixth floor and put their coats in his office closet. Then Reva led him out to the bank of security monitors across from the office.

Hank had just arrived, his eyes only half open, his blue store uniform crisp and unwrinkled. He was starting up the system, checking the monitors and VCRs, and seemed surprised to see Reva and her father come into his area.

"Morning," he said, staring at her questioningly.

"Hank, do you have the security tapes from yesterday?" Reva asked.

"Yeah. Sure," he said. "I was just rewinding them all. The police looked at them, but they don't show anything."

"Reva—what's this all about?" Mr. Dalby asked impatiently, straightening his striped tie.

"Hank, do you have a camera on the Santa Land area? Do you have a tape of that area from yesterday afternoon?" Reva asked, squeezing her father's hand as a signal for him to be patient.

"Yeah. Sure," Hank replied, mystified. "You want to see it?"

Reva nodded seriously, turning her eyes to the monitors.

"Reva—why do we have to look at Santa Claus?" Mr. Dalby demanded.

"I'm not sure," Reva said, her eyes on the screens. "I just have this idea. . . ."

A few seconds later one of the monitors began showing the Santa Land area. Reva moved closer to study the screen.

There was the store Santa with a little girl on his lap. He was ho-ho-hoing away. The girl was shy, reluctant to talk. After a while he lifted her off his lap and signaled to the elf to bring in the next child.

"Stop it right there," Reva instructed Hank.

The picture froze.

Reva studied the Santa's face.

"I'm right," she told her father. "I *knew* it. I'm right."

He waited for her to explain.

"It isn't Robb," she said. "It's someone else."

"Huh?" Hank exclaimed.

Mr. Dalby just stared at her, completely bewildered.

"That's not my friend Robb—even though he was supposed to be there. It's someone else. Someone Robb must have asked to cover for him."

"I don't understand," her father said, nervously fiddling with his tie. "Why would your friend do that?"

"I don't know," Reva said. "Maybe so he'd be free to kill Mitch. I—I really don't think Robb could do it. But it does seem a little suspicious, doesn't it?"

Her father nodded. "I guess," he said thoughtfully, staring at the frozen image on the screen.

"Michael actually gave me the idea," she told him excitedly.

"Michael?"

"After Michael sat on Santa's lap, he told me the Santa was a fake. He said Santa was wearing a pillow under his coat," Reva told him. "Well, I didn't think about it until the middle of the night. But then I remembered that Robb doesn't *wear* a pillow. He's a real chub. He doesn't *need* a pillow. So I realized that the Santa Michael talked to must have been someone else."

"But—that doesn't prove that Robb is a killer," Mr. Dalby said.

"Of course not," Reva replied. "But there's something else. Robb and Mitch had a serious fight that morning. A fistfight in the stockroom. I saw them. I tried to break it up. They were really going at it, trying to kill each other."

"Robb and Mitch?" Hank asked, surprised. "What were they fighting about?"

"I don't know," Reva replied. "Afterward, Mitch wouldn't tell me. But it was a really bad fight. Robb was really trying to take Mitch's head off."

"And then a few hours later Mitch was dead," Mr. Dalby said, thinking out loud.

"It was so weird," Reva said. "Robb is the quietest, most mild-mannered guy I know. He's always so sweet. I couldn't believe he was fighting like that. He was so angry at Mitch!"

"Angry enough to sneak off and kill him?" Hank asked.

Reva shrugged.

Her father stared hard at the picture on the monitor screen. "I'm calling the police," he said.

Since it was the last Saturday before Christmas, the store was jammed with shoppers from the time the doors opened. And even though it was early, there was already a line of twenty or thirty children, waiting impatiently for their big moment on Santa's lap.

Reva stood off to one side, her emotions swirling as she watched Robb deal with the kids. Maybe I'm wrong, she thought. Robb always seemed like such a teddy bear, sort of sad sometimes, but always nice. Is it really possible that he's a cold-blooded killer?

Maybe I'm wrong. It just doesn't seem possible.

It doesn't seem real. . . .

And it didn't seem real to Reva a few minutes later when four police officers descended on Santa's candy-striped throne. Robb had a little girl, dressed in bright orange sweatpants and matching sweatshirt, on his lap as the four grim-faced officers surrounded him. The little girl was angry. "It's my turn!" she shouted.

One of the police officers gently lifted the protesting girl off Robb's lap.

"What's going on?" Robb asked, very worried.

"Santa's being arrested!" an alarmed child called from the front of the line.

"Look—they're arresting Santa Claus!"

"What did Santa *do?*"

"Oh, no! Oh, no!"

"Stop them!"

"They can't arrest *Santa Claus!*"

The cries of astonished and alarmed children mixed with the hushed voices of their confused parents.

Two officers grabbed Robb by the arms and helped him up from the chair. One of them reached up and pulled off his beard.

Several children, still in line staring at the bizarre scene, gasped. A little boy burst into loud sobs.

"Are you Robb Spring?" one of the men demanded.

"Yes. But I didn't do anything!" Reva heard Robb exclaim over the cries of the distressed children and their parents.

"We'd like you to come with us. To answer some questions." The cop pulled Robb away from the garishly decorated throne. The other three stiffened, preparing themselves in case he resisted.

"But I didn't do anything!" Robb repeated fearfully.

"Are you going to come quietly with us?" the officer asked in a low, determined voice.

This is so awful, Reva thought, glancing at her father, who was watching from the line of children. He just shook his head.

Just then Reva felt herself being shoved aside as someone struggled past her. Regaining her balance, Reva was astonished to see her cousin Pam frantically rushing up to Robb.

"Foxy!" Pam cried. "What's happening? Why are they arresting you?"

Does Pam know Robb? Reva asked herself, surprised. Why is she calling him Foxy?

"Excuse us, miss." One of the officers tried to move Pam out of the way.

"Foxy—what's happening?" Pam demanded, dodging the policeman and grabbing the arm of Robb's Santa costume.

Foxy? Reva thought. That must be Pam's nickname for Robb.

"I only wanted to help you, Pam!" Robb cried emotionally.

"What?" Pam's face paled. "What did you do, Foxy? What did you *do?*"

"I only wanted to help you. I only wanted to get even!" Robb yelled, glaring past Pam to Reva.

What's he talking about? Reva wondered, suddenly chilled by Robb's wild, angry stare. Is Robb confessing?

Is he confessing that he killed Mitch?

"I only did it for you!" Robb told Pam.

"Foxy, I—I don't understand," Pam said weakly and covered her face with her hands. Mr. Dalby stepped forward and put his arm protectively around his niece.

The four officers led Robb away. "I only wanted to show Reva!" he screamed, turning his head back toward Pam, his red Santa cap falling to the floor. Then he and his dark-uniformed escorts disappeared down the short flight of stairs.

Parents began pulling their troubled children away from Santa Land. The area resounded with children's cries, angry adult voices, confused, nervous chatter.

Reva stood near the wall, oblivious of the noise and confusion, thinking hard, trying to figure out what Robb had meant.

He had screamed that he did what he did for Pam, that he only wanted to show Reva.

Show Reva what?

What could killing Mitch possibly show Reva?

Am *I* the cause of Mitch's death? Reva wondered. How can that *be*?

She looked across the now-empty aisle to where Pam was standing, staring at her, studying her.

Accusing her.

Chapter 27

THE DARK STORE,
AGAIN

*R*eva surprised herself by going back to the makeup counter and staying the rest of the day. She involved herself in the customers, listening to their demands, working hard, forcing herself not to think about anything that had happened.

Whenever there was even a brief lull, the frightening pictures would flash back into her mind. Pam's accusing stare. Robb's wild, terrified shouts. Mitch folded and bloody in the carton.

At least the murderer has been caught, Reva thought, consoling herself.

At least Robb was found out before he could kill again.

The day went by surprisingly fast. The store closed at seven. Reva's father had had to go to a meeting earlier in the afternoon, so she'd have to go home on the bus.

She stepped out through the employees' entrance into a clear, cold night. A half-moon was high in a purple-black sky.

She had started around to the bus stop at the front of the building, her shoes thudding on the narrow walkway, when she saw a figure half-hidden in the shadows, leaning against the building.

Waiting.

Waiting for me? Reva wondered.

Sudden fear made her stop.

The figure stepped quickly away from the building and approached Reva.

Reva took a step back, then froze.

"Pam!"

Her cousin, wearing only a raincoat, her hands buried in the pockets, came hurrying up to her.

"Pam, why are you still here?" Reva asked, relieved.

"Happy holidays," Pam said sadly. Her blond hair, normally tied back neatly, fell loosely about her shoulders. Her eyes, Reva saw, were bloodshot. It was obvious that she'd been crying. "I—I waited for you, Reva. I thought maybe you and I could talk." She stared at Reva expectantly, all the coldness, all the accusation gone from her eyes.

"Sure," Reva replied, studying Pam's troubled face.

"It's been so long since we really talked," Pam said quietly. "I mean, talked honestly."

Reva sighed. "Since Mom died," she whispered. Despite the cold night air, Reva was flooded with warm feelings, feelings for Pam, feelings that took her by surprise.

She took Pam's arm and began walking toward the front of the store.

"Listen, Reva," Pam said urgently, "Foxy—I mean, Robb—he couldn't have done it."

"Huh?"

"He couldn't have killed Mitch, Reva. No way," Pam said with real emotion. "I know him too well."

"I was shocked," Reva admitted. "I didn't think Robb could do it, either. But he must have, Pam."

"No!" Pam cried. She pulled her arm out of Reva's grip and stopped walking. "I'm telling you, Reva. It wasn't Robb. I know it!"

"But he was talking so crazy," Reva insisted. "He practically confessed this morning when they took him away."

"You don't understand—" Pam started.

"And I saw him fighting with Mitch yesterday morning," Reva interrupted. "I saw him, Pam. He wanted to kill Mitch. Really. And then later that afternoon he asked someone else to be Santa for him so he could sneak away."

"I can explain everything," Pam declared. "There's my dad's car over there." She pointed to the hulking Grand Prix at the curb. "Please, Reva. Let's sit down, get out of the cold. Let me explain. Give me a chance."

"Of course," Reva said. She followed Pam to the big old car and climbed into the passenger seat. It smelled old, sour.

"I know why Foxy was fighting with Mitch," Pam said, sliding behind the wheel, starting to talk before she had even slammed the door. "It was my fault."

"Your fault?"

"Foxy knew that Mitch was blackmailing me," Pam revealed. "That's why he was fighting with Mitch."

Reva's mouth formed an O of surprise. "Huh? Mitch? Blackmailing you? Come on, Pam. Why?"

Pam hesitated. She rested her forehead on the wheel for a few seconds before sitting up again. "It's too long a story, Reva. I'm sure it'll all come out. But later. Right now, I want to talk about Foxy—I mean, Robb."

Reva eyed Pam suspiciously. What is it she doesn't want to tell me? she wondered. Why would Mitch be blackmailing her?

"So why did Robb ask someone to take his place as Santa?" she asked.

"It's all very innocent, really," Pam said, sighing. "He got a friend of his to stand in for him for an hour so he could see me."

"You?"

"Robb and I have been going together for nearly six months. He knew I was very upset about . . . things. So he sneaked off to see me. Just to be with me."

Reva knew Pam was telling the truth.

But there were still things to be explained.

"What was he saying when the police took him away, Pam?" Reva asked. "What did he mean that he was only trying to show me?"

"Foxy told me that he had been doing mean things

to frighten you. Playing cruel jokes. He said he put a needle in your lipstick. And he sent you things. A cologne bottle. A mannequin in a box. I told him it was silly. But he was just so angry at the way you treated me, at how awful you were to me. And at how you tricked him into being Santa Claus, how you humiliated him in front of everyone."

Reva avoided Pam's eyes.

"But that's all he did," Pam continued. "You've *got* to believe me. He didn't kill Mitch. I know he didn't. I know he couldn't."

Reva saw that Pam had tears in her eyes, and to Reva's surprise, she did too. "You had a right to be angry at me," she told her cousin, her voice a whisper. "Robb did too. I guess . . . I guess a lot of people do."

Then with sincere feeling, Reva reached over to Pam, threw both arms around her shoulders, and wrapped her tightly in a long hug. "I'm really sorry, Pam. Really. I'm so sorry," she said.

"Can I drive you home?" Pam asked, tears rolling down her cheeks. "I want to call to find out what happened to Foxy."

"Yes, thanks," Reva said. "Maybe you could stay for dinner, and we could talk. You know. Catch up."

"Maybe," Pam said, searching for her car keys.

They were two or three blocks away when Reva realized she didn't have her bag. "I must have left it up in Daddy's office," she told Pam apologetically. "Can we go back and get it?"

Pam made a U-turn at the next light. When they reached the store, Reva directed her around the back to the employees' entrance. "Wait right here," she told Pam. "I'll be down in two seconds."

Reva stepped into the narrow corridor, surprised to see that the night guard wasn't at his table. Daddy wouldn't be pleased about that, she thought.

She walked quickly through the dark, empty back hallway and stepped out onto the main floor, her eyes searching the darkened store. Except for some pale ceiling lamps against the far wall, the only light came from the twinkling tree lights on the tall Christmas tree under the balconies.

Chill out. Just chill out, she warned herself, feeling her old fear begin to return. Just a suggestion of the terror she always felt, a heaviness in the pit of her stomach. But she knew it would soon spread. The fear would soon spread until it had her in its grip.

Stupid phobia.

Chill out, Reva. There's nothing to be frightened of.

What was that music? Reva stopped to listen. Someone had left the music system on. "Silent Night" echoed eerily through the empty store.

The Christmas tree lights still on. The music still playing. No guard at the back door. Someone had been careless, Reva decided. It's a good thing Daddy's not here. He'd make someone pay for these slipups.

The fear tried to push her back, keep her frozen in the center of the aisle. But with the soft Christmas music in her ears, she forced herself forward. She held her breath until she reached the employees' elevator, then slipped inside and rode up to the sixth floor.

She stepped out into the executive waiting room,

feeling relieved, feeling proud of herself for not allowing the fear to overwhelm her.

Moving quickly over the plush carpet, she hurried toward her father's office in the corner. To her surprise, the security monitors were still on, their screens buzzing, filled now with nothing but gray.

What's going on around here? she wondered.

And then she saw that someone was standing at the monitors.

"Hank?" she called, moving toward him. "Hank— what are you doing here so—?"

It wasn't Hank.

The man who stepped out from behind the bank of monitors was wearing a blue security guard's uniform. The buzzing, gray screens washed him in gray so that he seemed unreal, a strange video creation.

Staring into the gray glare, it took Reva a long while to recognize him.

"Mr. Wakely!" she cried, and then in her surprise she blurted out, "You don't work here anymore!"

"I still have some work to do," he said.

Then Reva saw the pistol in his hand.

Chapter 28

"TAKE IT EASY, MR. WAKELY"

*T*he chorus singing "Silent Night" over the loud-speakers seemed to get louder.

Reva's mouth dropped open as her eyes traveled from the pistol up to Mr. Wakely's face, gray in the light from the monitor screens.

He took a step toward her. Then another.

His natural color returned. His eyes were red and glassy, Reva noticed. She could see red veins on the bridge of his bulbous nose.

"Maywood promised me there'd be no problem," he said, his eyes floating from side to side in their sockets.

He's drunk, Reva realized, returning her open-eyed stare to the pistol gripped tightly in his hand.

Drunk and dangerous.

"Maywood promised me," he repeated. Maybe he wanted to explain his presence to Reva.

"Take it easy, Mr. Wakely," she said, holding up her hands. "Just stay calm, okay. I'm sure everything will be all right." Her heart was pounding so loudly, she could barely hear her own words.

"No." He shook his head. "It didn't go all right. We messed up. We completely messed up." He was slurring his words so badly, Reva had trouble understanding him.

"What do you mean?" she asked, still gripped with fear.

"The robbery. Maywood. He was the one who planned it. He said there wouldn't be any trouble." He took a step back and put a hand out against the side of a monitor and leaned against it.

"You mean the robbery here in the store?" Reva asked.

He nodded, his bald head shining gray in the strange light. "Maywood said that three kids were planning to rob the store. He said the three kids would be a distraction. You know. Keep the other guard busy. Me and Maywood would empty the downstairs safe, see. And the three kids wouldn't even know it."

He paused as if trying to remember what happened next. Then he continued, training his red eyes on Reva. "We got the money okay. It was a good plan, see. It would've worked fine. Only I stepped out from the back office, and I saw that one of the kids was *mine!*"

He shook his head sadly. "It was Mickey. My own boy. I had no idea." His eyes burned into hers, pleading, desperate. "Maywood never said that Mickey was one of them. I didn't know that Mickey was there. He didn't know that I was there. And then . . ."

He trailed off, rubbing his chin with his free hand.

"And then what?" Reva asked, checking for the safest escape route.

"Then . . . I saw the guard. Ed Javors. He picked up his gun. He was going to shoot Mickey. What could I do? I'm a father, right? I couldn't stand there and let him shoot my son. My only son? So I—I just panicked. I shot Ed. I didn't mean to kill him. But I couldn't let him shoot Mickey."

He stopped again, lost in thought, leaning hard against the monitor.

On the loudspeaker the chorus continued its soft, reverent version of "Silent Night."

"Did you kill Mitch too?" Reva asked. The question just popped out of her.

Mr. Wakely nodded. "Had to," he said, trying to focus his eyes. "I knew what he was doing. I overheard, see. He was blackmailing my kid. That kid Mitch was out back the night of the robbery. He'd gone back to the store for something he left there. He saw Mickey and the other two come running out. And so he started blackmailing my boy. Going to turn him in. I couldn't allow it, could I? I couldn't allow Mickey to get into trouble for something I did."

"But why did you send Mitch's body to me?" Reva asked, staring at the pistol, still down at his side.

"Huh?" He squinted at her, as if that would help him understand the question. "Send it to you? I didn't. I found a big carton with a bow on it. First big carton I could find. So I put the body in it and left it behind a counter," he told her.

The carton that had the mannequin in it, Reva realized. It still had her name on it, and it had gotten delivered to her all over again.

Mr. Wakely squinted at her. "And now here I am. I came back to finish my work here, see. I just want to get paid, see. From the safe in your daddy's office." He gestured toward the office with the pistol.

"Too bad," he said, standing up straight. His eyes seemed to be focusing now, clear and cold. He raised the pistol. "You've given me no choice."

"No!" Reva screamed and whirled around to run.

Her legs felt as if they weighed a thousand pounds. But she forced herself forward, bending low as she ran, her entire body tensed in anticipation of the gunshots.

He was coming after her, the pistol poised. She could hear his heavy breathing, hear the heavy pad of his shoes on the thick carpet.

What can I do? Where can I go? she wondered, the empty offices flying by in a blur.

If I could just get onto the elevator—

No. Too risky. Too slow.

Then where?

If she could double back to her father's office, she could lock the door, lock herself in, call out for help.

Yes.

But how could she get past him to get back there?

No time to think about it. No time to make a plan. She just had to do it.

She reached the waiting room, circled the couch, took a deep breath, and ran right at him.

His mouth dropped open in surprise.

Don't shoot. Don't shoot. Don't shoot.

She dodged past him, running hard, running at full speed.

It took her a while to realize that the object that rang past her ear was a bullet.

"Oh!" She uttered a terrified cry.

Another explosion behind her, this one louder, this one scarier since she knew what it was. Another bullet rang past, lodging in the wall ahead of her.

Reva froze.

Her father's office was still halfway down the hall.

I can't outrun a bullet, she thought.

And then her thoughts seemed to melt into bright colors, unconnected words, a loud, insistent ringing in her ears as her panic drove out everything else.

She backed up toward the low balcony overlooking the store.

Her back hit the railing. She didn't really know where she was. She didn't really know why she had stopped, why she was standing there, what she was doing.

A grim smile on his face, the smoking pistol held high, Wakely dived at her.

Chapter 29

ZAP

*H*e's got me, Reva thought, her back pressed against the low chrome balcony railing.

She glanced down, down to the main floor five stories below, and felt overcome by dizziness.

He leapt, arms outstretched, to tackle her.

She shut her eyes and ducked.

Wakely sailed past her—and plunged over the balcony.

She could hear him scream all the way down.

Then she heard the clatter of glass, a cracking sound, a low cry, a hard thud.

And then a deafening, final scream followed by an electrical *zap-zap-zap*, and a roar that seemed to shake the walls.

Reva peered down to the first floor. She cried out, raising her hands to her face, when she saw Wakely down there, his eyes frozen open in a wide stare of horror, his body being jolted in the midst of a blinding red and yellow electric current.

It's the Christmas tree, Reva realized, still covering her face, turning away from the horrifying sight.

Wakely had landed on the tree, and it shorted out.

Reva felt sick.

She heard a last few *pop-pop-pops,* like automatic gunshots, and then the current fizzled out.

"Ohh," she moaned softly.

And suddenly someone was holding her. Strong arms were around her, supporting her, comforting her.

"Hank!"

"I was downstairs, fixing a videocam," he said softly, holding her tighter. "I saw everything. On the monitor in the basement. It's all on tape. Wakely's confession, everything."

She raised her head from his chest and met his eyes, still dazed. "Huh? How?"

"I told you I was an electronics genius," he said. "I tried to get up here to help you. Sorry I couldn't get here sooner."

"At least you're here now," Reva said weakly. And then she collapsed into his arms.

Chapter 30

REAL FEELINGS

Reva sat between Hank and Robb on the long wooden bench. They huddled together, hunched in their coats, collars up, squinting against the bright glare of the lights above them.

Footsteps echoed on the marble floors, and from time to time a door would open and a uniformed police officer would hurry past.

Reva and the two boys had been sitting outside the Shadyside police hearing room for nearly an hour, staring at the tile walls, not talking much, nervously waiting for Pam to come out.

"What's it like in there?" Hank asked Robb, gesturing to the tall double doors that led inside.

"It's not bad," Robb said, shivering. "It's warmer than out here."

"The North Pole is warmer than out here," Reva cracked, holding on to the arm of Hank's overcoat.

"There are a bunch of little rooms back there," Robb said. "With chairs and desks and stuff. That's all."

"And one-way mirrors, right?" Hank asked. "So they can spy on you?"

Robb chuckled. "I don't think so. I didn't see any mirrors at all."

"How long were you in there?" Reva asked, glancing expectantly at the door, then checking her wristwatch.

"About an hour. Maybe a little more," Robb replied. "I was scared. But I knew I hadn't done anything wrong." He blushed. "Except for those mean things I did to you."

"I deserved it," Reva said softly. Then she laughed. "Besides, I'll find a way to pay you back. It's my turn."

Robb became concerned. "You're joking—right?"

Reva nodded slyly. "Maybe."

They sat in silence for a while, staring at the double doors, willing them to open. Reva gripped Hank's hand tightly. "What do you think will happen to Pam?"

Hank shrugged.

The doors opened.

Pam came walking out, weary and pale, flanked by her somber parents. She brightened a little when she saw Reva and the two boys waiting for her.

They jumped to their feet as Pam and her parents approached, their footsteps echoing in the high-ceilinged waiting room.

"Pam—what happened?" Reva asked, hurrying to her.

Pam shrugged and glanced back at her mom and dad. "There's going to be a hearing," she said. "In the meantime, I'm in my parents' custody."

"Custody?" Reva exclaimed. "What a horrible word."

"Pam's going to be okay," her father said brusquely.

"She's never been in trouble before," her mother added. "So they're only going to charge her with trespassing."

"And what about Mickey and Clay?" Robb asked.

"I don't know," Pam said, shaking her head sadly. "Mickey's hearing won't be until after his father's funeral. He's staying with his aunt. Clay's hearing is next week."

They all walked out the door and down the steps of the police station. A light snow had begun to fall, tiny, wet flakes that tickled Reva's nose and felt good on her cheeks. The sidewalk and ground were already white. She searched for the moon, but it was covered by clouds.

Holding Hank's hand, Reva glanced at Pam on her other side. Pam smiled at her, and Reva stopped, turned away from Hank, and gave Pam a long hug.

I feel so warm, Reva thought, so light, as if a layer of ice had melted away from me. If I hadn't been so cold, so bottled up, so hateful, maybe none of this would have happened.

What a shame that such horrors had to take place

before I could feel again, Reva thought. Now she felt sadness, and relief that it was all over.

I have real feelings now, she realized. Warm feelings. Sad feelings.

Silently she made a New Year's resolution to herself never to lose those feelings again.

Then, leaning against Hank, she walked with the others through the silent night into the soft falling snow.

About the Author

R. L. STINE is the author of more than twenty mysteries and thrillers for Young Adult readers. He also writes funny novels and joke books.

In addition to his publishing work, he is Head Writer of the children's TV show, "Eureeka's Castle."

He lives in New York City with his wife, Jane, and son, Matt.

WATCH OUT FOR

FEAR STREET®

THE KNIFE

Laurie Masters loves her job as a student volunteer at Shadyside Hospital—until weird things start to happen on the Children's Floor. Soon it becomes clear that someone doesn't want Laurie snooping around—and will do anything to get rid of her! The terrifying trail Laurie follows leads to deception, cold-blooded murder and, ultimately, to Fear Street!

FEAR STREET®

R.L. Stine

- THE NEW GIRL ....74649-9/$3.99
- THE SURPRISE PARTY ....73561-6/$3.99
- THE OVERNIGHT ....74650-2/$3.99
- MISSING ....69410-3/$3.99
- THE WRONG NUMBER .....69411-1/$3.99
- THE SLEEPWALKER ....74652-9/$3.99
- HAUNTED ....74651-0/$3.99
- HALLOWEEN PARTY ....70243-2/$3.99
- THE STEPSISTER ....70244-0/$3.99
- SKI WEEKEND ....72480-0/$3.99
- THE FIRE GAME ....72481-9/$3.99
- THE THRILL CLUB ....78581-8/$3.99

- LIGHTS OUT ....72482-7/$3.99
- THE SECRET BEDROOM .....72483-5/$3.99
- THE KNIFE ....72484-3/$3.99
- THE PROM QUEEN ....72485-1/$3.99
- FIRST DATE ....73865-8/$3.99
- THE BEST FRIEND ....73866-6/$3.99
- THE CHEATER ....73867-4/$3.99
- SUNBURN ....73868-2/$3.99
- THE NEW BOY ....73869-0/$3.99
- THE DARE ....73870-4/$3.99
- BAD DREAMS ....78569-9/$3.99
- DOUBLE DATE ....78570-2/$3.99
- ONE EVIL SUMMER ....78596-6/$3.99

FEAR STREET SAGA

- #1: THE BETRAYAL ....86831-4/$3.99
- #2: THE SECRET ....86832-2/$3.99
- #3: THE BURNING ......86833-0/$3.99

SUPER CHILLER

- PARTY SUMMER ......72920-9/$3.99
- BROKEN HEARTS .....78609-1/$3.99
- THE DEAD LIFEGUARD ....86834-9/$3.99

CHEERLEADERS

- THE FIRST EVIL ....75117-4/$3.99
- THE SECOND EVIL ....75118-2/$3.99
- THE THIRD EVIL ....75119-0/$3.99

99 FEAR STREET: THE HOUSE OF EVIL

- THE FIRST HORROR ....88562-6/$3.99
- THE SECOND HORROR ....88563-4/$3.99
- THE THIRD HORROR ....88564-2/$3.99

Simon & Schuster Mail Order
200 Old Tappan Rd., Old Tappan, N.J. 07675

Please send me the books I have checked above. I am enclosing $_____ (please add $0.75 to cover the postage and handling for each order. Please add appropriate sales tax). Send check or money order–no cash or C.O.D.'s please. Allow up to six weeks for delivery. For purchase over $10.00 you may use VISA: card number, expiration date and customer signature must be included.

Name _____

Address _____

City _____ State/Zip _____

VISA Card # _____ Exp.Date _____

Signature _____

739-16